STEEL TOE REVIEW
Contemporary Southern Arts and Literature

Volume 3

Copyright © 2014 Steel Toe Review and Tritone Media
All Rights Reserved

Published by
Tritone Media
5751 9th Avenue South
Birmingham, AL 35212

Cover design by John Lytle Wilson
Illustrations by Stephen Smith, TK, TK
Layout by M. David Hornbuckle

Please visit our website: www.steeltoereview.com

Steel Toe Review: Volume 3
ISBN 978-0-9849495-2-6

Printed in the USA
First printing March 2013
e d c b a

STEEL TOE REVIEW
Contemporary Southern Arts and Literature

Volume 3

Compiled by the Editors of Steel Toe Review

New York ◆ Birmingham

Table of Contents

Fiction

"Daryl and Pete-O Go to Walmart" by Cathy Adams 3
"Tips" by Lis Anna 14
"Resurrection Fern" by CL Bledsoe 27
"Echoes and Starch" by Justin Brouckaert 34
"Like a Bull" by Katie Burgess 53
"Like a Burst of Fire" by Jackson Culpepper 58
"Grounded" by Tyler Dennis 67
"Deep Sea Fishing" by Brenna Dixon 80
"Periscope (Hart Crane)" by Lauren Eyler 101
"Damage" by Jody Hobbs Hesler 115
"Offender" by Christopher Lowe 136
"Vietnam. Fucking Vietnam" by William Trent Pancoast 140

Essays

"The Real Thing: My Life in Coke" by Deborah Gold 107
"Kerry" by Ian Hoppe 128

Poetry

"For Sandy, Who Never Got Her Dance" by Maari Carter 9
"For My Mother, Who Didn't Provide a Forwarding Address" by Maari Carter 10
"Waffle House Rhapsody" by Maari Carter 12
"Light on Rust" by Tobi Cogswell 21
"Tired, Can't Sleep, Want Drink, Need Hug" by Tobi Cogswell 22
"At Altitude" by Tobi Cogswell 23
"Abalone" by Tobi Cogswell 25
"How Jo-Beth Came to Love the Sky" by Tobi Cogswell 26
"Tongue Economics" by John Davis, Jr 33
"One Block Off Bourbon" by Matt Dennison 51
"A Difference" by Matt Dennison 52

"Melancholy" by Michael Diebert 55
"Lightning Bugs" by Michael Diebert 56
"Letter to Ferris from Decatur" by Michael Diebert 57
"Three Stanzas for Luis J. Rodriguez" by Mario Duarte 65
"101 Degrees" by Mario Duarte 65
"Locked Trunk to Trunk" by Mario Duarte 66
"Post-Exorcism Lunchroom Fugue" by Brandi George 74
"Poems Burnt In a Trash Barrel" by Brandi George 75
"Driving Home From Choir Practice" by Brandi George 78
"Night Jetty" by Hastings Hensel 96
"Conversion Narrative in a Walk-In Freezer" by Hastings Hensel 97
"Snag Arrangement" by Hastings Hensel 98
"Widowmaker" by Hastings Hensel 99
"Bycatch" by Hastings Hensel 100
"How the Moose Fell in Snow" by Donald Illich 106
"An Offering" by Ray McManus 114
"Last Course" by Claire McQuerry 123
"Stratigraphy" by Claire McQuerry 125
"Settlement" by Claire McQuerry 126
"Fibonacci for the Life List" by Karla Linn Merrifield 135
"Going Through a Period of Periods" by Karla Linn Merrifield 135
"To the Trailer" by Emily Porter 138
"The Kitchen Floor" by Colleen Powderly 143
"Ax" by Esteban Rodriguez 144
"Calf" by Esteban Rodriguez 145
"Cats" by Esteban Rodriguez 145
"Ghost" by Anna Lowe Weber 146

For Chad, Joey, and Craig

Editor's Note
M. David Hornbuckle

Welcome to the third print issue of Steel Toe Review.

When Chad King handed me my copy of his first solo album *Follow Me Home*, he said I should listen to the album on a very hot summer day with my windows down so a cool breeze could waft through. I suggest you read this issue under similar conditions, preferably while lying in a hammock and sipping on a fresh mint julep. I know... mint juleps are so cliché Southern, but they are so good. It is one of those things about our Southern identity that I completely embrace. So set up your hammock, and go pick some fresh Kentucky Colonel mint form the garden. We'll wait...

All set now? Good.

This issue is obviously our best yet. During the past year, we increased our advertising, which dramatically increased our exposure and our submissions. Subsequently, we tripled our staff to keep up with all the reading. It has been quite a year.

We are a little behind schedule in getting this out, but we are here now, and we are thankful for that. We are also thankful to the following people who donated to our Kickstarter campaign and made this book possible, in no particular order: Chip Brantley, Nancy Rutland Glaub, Mary Bast, Kerry Freeman, Rita Bourke, Burgin Matthews, John Troutman, Jeannette Brown, Jon & Mary Anne Hornbuckle, Susan Weinberg, Christopher Saady, Ray McManus, Aimee Noonan, Kyle Cornelius, Shan Sheik, John Saad, Harriet Godwin, Melford Wilson, Philip Theibert, Gisele Laterrade, Kerry Madden-Lunsford, and Daniel Taylor.

A number of these donors have been a part of the STR community since we began, and some have been published in previous issues. The longing for this type of community is one of the reasons we started this project in the first place, back in October 2010. We wanted a way to directly connect the community of writers in Birmingham with other writers all over the world. By publishing a magazine that makes an effort to include talent connected to Birmingham, but open to anyone, we hoped to make those connections. We think the experiment has proven quite successful so far.

I personally want to thank our excellent staff for helping curate this collection: Matt Layne, Mike Tesney, Callie Mauldin, Halley Cotton, Cheyenne Taylor, and Jason Walker. I also want to thank the cover artist John Lytle Wilson, the illustrator Stephen Smith, and all the authors who have supported us for the past three-plus years.

Enjoy that julep, sit back, and sip on some good writing!

- M. David Hornbuckle

Daryl and Pete-O Go to Walmart
Cathy Adams

Pete-O was fairly disgusting even before he lost his legs. He didn't actually lose them. They were cut off by a doctor when his diabetes got so bad it was going to kill him. Pete-O was really fat and smelled like turnip greens. He spent the whole weekend bitching about having to get his legs cut off before he went to the hospital on Monday. We went with him because Mama said that's what family was supposed to do. I thought she meant that we were going to have to watch him getting his legs sawed off like they do in TV shows when people stand way up above somebody in surgery in a glass room so they can look down at what's happening. The thought of seeing a man's legs getting sawed off made me pretty excited, so I told all my friends that I was going to watch. When it turned out that we didn't get to see anything but we just had to sit in plastic chairs in a waiting room, I was pissed. For about an hour I sat there fuming at Mama, even though she didn't really lie to me. She never told me we'd see his legs get cut off. I was just hoping.

Losing his legs left Pete-O angry all the time, even angrier than he'd been before, and he was usually in a bad mood even when he had both legs. We went over to his house a lot because he couldn't do much for himself, and he was so mad at everybody and everything he didn't want to try. "You just got to stop feeling sorry for yourself," Mama would say, and then their sister Norva would say the same thing, "Yeah, you got to stop feeling sorry for yourself." Whatever Mama would say Norva would repeat it like that until I wondered if Pete-O was going to just start crawling on the floor to get away from the two them. That's what I would do if I had sisters like that to listen to every day. I could run outside in the yard when people started getting on my nerves, but Pete-O just had to sit there in his wheelchair, or worse, lie there in his bed and listen to his sisters drive him crazy. He was too fat to move himself. He had to get help doing every little thing, and that was what Mama and Aunt Norva were there for, them and some nurses who came by every day to help with stuff. I don't really know what they did because I always went outside as soon as they came around. It was one day when they were there that I found the puppy. He was solid brown all over and fat, and his feet were muddy like he'd been walking a long way before he showed up hiding under a yellow bell bush in Pete-O's neighbor's yard. I knew all the dogs around Pete-O's house, and this one didn't belong to anybody. I figured somebody dumped him on the road because he was scared and shaking when he crawled under that bush to get a better look. I talked real soft to him and he let me pet him until I could get my hand underneath his belly to pull him out. At first I thought I'd take him home with me, but Mama was all the time threatening to shoot the three we had because they were always getting into her flowers and pulling sheets off the line and stuff. This puppy was warm, he liked having his ears scratched, he smelled like bologna, and he needed a home, so I decided that Pete-O should have him.

At first Mama frowned when I held the puppy up to her and told her he was a present for Uncle Pete-O. "He's probably full of worms," she said.

"Uh-huh, probably got worms," said Norva, pointing a finger at the dog from behind Mama.

"He ain't got worms. Lookit how fat he is," I said. Mama didn't look like she was going to change her mind. I had to think fast. "We got wormer at home. I'll give him some and he'll be fine."

"Who's going to let him outside to pee? That dog'll make a mess of Pete-O's carpets," said Mama.

"A real mess of the carpet," said Norva.

"Bring it here," said Pete-O from inside his bedroom. That shut Mama and Norva up, so I ran the three steps into his room, holding the puppy.

"Put him down here a minute. Let me see him," said Pete-O. He pushed himself a little straighter against his pillows and leaned forward to take a look. The little dog took a few steps towards him, leaving dirty paw prints on the clean sheets Mama had put down the day before. Pete-O put a meaty hand on the dog's back and rubbed his fur. He began nodding. "Go get that wormer and get him cleaned up."

That settled it and the dog was his. Pete-O named him Daryl after his favorite character on *The Walking Dead*, and Daryl became his favorite companion. Pete-O told everybody that Daryl was his guide dog, and later, when Pete-O got one of those special vans for handicapped people and started driving himself around town, Daryl was with him everywhere he went. I think most people knew that Daryl wasn't really a guide dog, but nobody said anything. I found out later that Pete-O had told a few people who didn't know him that he had lost his legs in the Gulf War, and besides that, he always wore a "God Bless America" cap with a flag pin stuck in the side. Nobody's going to tell a man who'd had his legs blown off in Afghanistan that he can't bring his dog with him into the Waffle House or the grocery store. I got him a "Proud to be an American" bumper sticker for the back of his wheelchair just to help shut people up.

Pete-O was still pretty disgusting. He liked to spit out the window of his van when he was driving, and sometimes he had crumbs and crap in his beard because he was always eating Little Debbie cupcakes or those orange waffle cookies that smell like cardboard. I spent a lot of time looking out the window of the van when he was talking to me just so I wouldn't have to see his face up close, but he was the only uncle I had who would take me anywhere I wanted to go. So, I hung out with him at least once a week. Besides, Daryl was always with us and I loved being with Darryl. He ate the same things Pete-O did, and sometimes he had orange crap hanging from his mouth too, but somehow it didn't seem so disgusting on a dog.

When Pete-O bought a pistol he let me go with him on Thursdays after school to the shooting range. Mama and Norva were just glad he had taken an interest in something and was getting out more. Mama even decided that Daryl hadn't been such a bad idea. Pete-O and I would leave Daryl in the van with the windows rolled down a little so he wouldn't get too hot. He'd stick his head out and bark like a fool at the shooting until we were done. I got pretty good at hitting the target, better than Pete-O. I figured he was having some eye problems because his diabetes was getting worse, but he loved to go shooting about as much as anything. Pete-O would sit up as tall as he could in his wheelchair, take aim with his left eye squinted shut and say, "Here's yours, you son-of-a-bitch," right before he squeezed off a few rounds. One day I asked him who he was talking about, and he said, "Son, there's a new one every week," and then he started laughing. I laughed with him because I thought I was supposed to, but I didn't know what he thought was funny.

On the Thursday that everything happened we stopped at Walmart like we did every week after we went to the shooting range so we could both get a Coke slush. They weren't really made of Coca-cola, but that was just what Uncle Pete-O called it, and it was our favorite treat after an hour or two of target practice. I liked the green and purple flavors mixed and Pete-O liked the orange. His lips turned orange when he drank it and he dribbled some in his beard, so I made sure I kept my eyes on Daryl. Daryl didn't like Coke slushes, so we bought him a wiener from the hot box on the counter. Pete-O put it on the table so it could cool down enough for Daryl to eat it. He really cared about Daryl like that. All Daryl could do was stare at that wiener like it was the last thing he was ever going to eat. His whole face was quivering and he kept licking the slobber from his lips, waiting for Pete-O to hand it to him. "Look at him," said Pete-O, and he was smiling. "Nothing he likes better than a hotdog," he said, reaching down and stroking Daryl's back as the dog wolfed down the meat. Pete-O picked up his drink, shook the contents, and sucked hard on the straw until there was nothing but air. We were nearly through when the man came up to us. His hands were on his hips, and for some reason it made me think of Mama, the way he was standing there with his lips all curled in like he was going tell me to go pick up the dirty clothes on my floor or clean up the kitchen counter where I'd left a mess from making a sandwich. It was a stupid thought, but it was the first thing that crossed my mind.

"Sir, I'm afraid the dog will have to go outside," said the man. He wasn't wearing one of those vests like the other people at Walmart wear, the one with the smiley faces on it. He was wearing a white shirt with a tie, and he had a company nametag that said Randall. His hair was combed over his head real neat like he had just got his hair cut. He was a manager, and from the look of his clean nametag, he must have just been promoted because I'd never seen him on any of the Thursdays Pete-O and I had been in the snack bar after target practice.

"Maybe you're not paying attention," said Pete-O. He pushed his wheelchair from our handicapped accessible table a little and let Randall see his legs, or I guess where his legs used to be.

"Yessir, I can see your situation, but dogs are not allowed in the store. He'll have to go."

"My what?" asked Pete-O, and he chuckled enough that his plaid shirt shook over his belly just a little, but it was an irritated sound, not the kind of chuckle you make when something is funny. "Did you say 'my situation'?"

"I sympathize with your handicap, sir. My own brother was in Iraq and came back without his left hand, but be that as it may, the dog has to go."

"Well, be that as it may," mocked Pete-O, "my dog happens to be a guide dog, and your policy says that he can be here."

"That policy is for trained service dogs, and this dog does not have proper identification to be a service dog," said Randall, dropping his hands from his hips.

"Proper identification?" This time Pete-O did let out a laugh, and I did, too. Anybody could see that expecting a dog to have an I.D. card like a driver's license was plain funny. "You hear that? This guy thinks Daryl oughta have identification, like he's some kind of police officer or something." Daryl had been sitting back on his haunches throughout this entire conversation, but the conversation was getting loud and he must have figured something wasn't right because he stood up on all fours and got real still.

"Service dogs have vests and their owners have papers," said Randall, his voice growing terser.

"Well guess what?" said Pete-O, his voice rising. "I don't have papers. All I got is this," and he pointed to his head. I wasn't sure if he meant that he had a brain or if he was pointing to the God Bless America and the tiny flag pin on the front of his cap. "And this is all I need. We still live in a free country, or at least we're supposed to. But all people like you can do is to take our rights away one by one that men fought and died for, and you think we'll just sit back and take it."

"Sir, this is Walmart and the dog has to go outside," said Randall. Two women had entered the snack area and were loitering near the next table, listening.

"It's a sorry state when a crippled vet and his dog can't even sit in a Walmart and have a cold drink," said Pete-O.

"You ain't no vet." I hadn't meant to say it. The words just came out, and from the way Pete-O glared at me I was sure he was never going to take me shooting again. I was as ashamed as I'd ever been in my life. I knew Pete-O was lying, but saying what I did like that in front of everybody made me want to throw up my Coke slush.

Pete-O was still glaring at me when he answered the manager. "It don't matter one bit if I'm a vet or not! My dog is as much a service dog as any blind person's with one of those fancy vests. He can bring me a magazine and he even knows how to turn on the faucet in the bathtub."

I was pretty sure he was lying about the turning on the faucet part, but one time

I had seen Daryl pick up a Guns and Ammo magazine off the floor and carry it to Pete-O. I found my chance to try and make Pete-O less mad at me about the vet thing. "That's right," I said, "and he can even dial the telephone." Pete-O looked a little surprised, but he didn't try to say it wasn't true. The part about the phone was a lie, a big lie, but I thought that guy Randall deserved it, and I couldn't wait to tell Mama this story. She'd think it was funny when I told her what I said about Daryl and the telephone. Everybody would. I was smiling a little to myself when I thought about telling the story to everybody as soon as we got home later that night.

"If you don't leave with the dog, I'm going to have to call the police," said Randall.

"Is that a fact?"

"Yessir, that's a fact," said Randall.

Pete-O's lips pressed together and he reached into his pocket. His hand fumbled around for a second, and when he pulled it out again he was holding his pistol. He pointed it straight up at Randall. All the air in my mouth got sucked down my throat and I couldn't let go of my Coke slush. "You want to call the police," said Pete-O, "you go ahead. It's the last thing you'll ever do."

"Now, now, just a minute. . ." Randall took a step backwards, his hands out in front of him as if he thought was going to shield himself from a bullet.

Pete-O cocked his pistol. "Here's yours, you son-of-a-bitch," and then he fired. Blood spread over Randall's stomach like a big flower had exploded under his shirt. There was screaming, but it sounded like it was coming from far away. My whole body felt numb, and I couldn't move as I watched Pete-O put his wheelchair in reverse and begin backing away from the table. He was saying something to me, calling my name, but I didn't really hear him. I could see his mouth opening in front of me over and over, but I just sat there while Randall fell to the floor where Daryl had been standing just a minute before. Or at least it seemed like a minute. Pete-O turned his wheelchair around and started driving away from me with Daryl trotting along behind him. I watched the two of them disappear down the aisle that ran next to the Halloween costumes and candy. I don't know how long I sat there. I just know that the screaming didn't stop the whole time I was at that little table, squeezing my cup until it busted open in my hand.

When I caught up to them in the doorway it was all over. Pete-O was in handcuffs, still sitting in his wheelchair. Police were all around him, and there was a wall of people trying to get a look but they were held back by another wall of some cops and some employees with smiley faces on their vests. I heard from somebody later that Pete-O had handed his gun over to the police without a word. He must have spotted me because he called my name and everybody started looking over at me, especially the cops. "Take Daryl," Pete-O called, and then the police started pushing his wheelchair toward the big entrance doors.

Somebody had put a leash on Daryl, and one of the police officers was holding it out to me to come and take it. Daryl had that same scared look he'd had the day I found him under the bush. I put my hand on his head and he was trembling. Pete turned his head around right as they were pushing him out the big sliding doors. He was smiling the same smile he had when he was at the shooting range, like he was in charge of everything and somebody was going to get his.

Illustration by Stephen Smith

For Sandy, Who Never Got Her Dance
Maari Carter

What you're told: *it was rat poison,*
a little more and she'd have thrown it up. Instead

her mother decorates her grave out in Carrollton
at Hickory Grove every Christmas, has for the last

forty years. So you go, because you're fifteen
and there are worse traditions than a dead girl

who wanted a boy's damp hand against her back
before he deployed, had only meant it enough

to scare them, make them regret not letting her go.
What you're not told: this is only one version

of grief, and its electricity haunts the pine thicket;
the injustice in re-hanging wreaths

older than a person feels like a *fuck you*
to the chances of days, the accidental graze

of life's sweet ass and songs even stars dance to—
that you'll want to burn it, the dented

reindeer antlers each inch of limp garland, the guestbook,
filled with names who came flaunting their pulses—

that you won't understand how headlights
can be desperate, how for every bloodflooded chest

there's a gymnasium, with cardboard cutout stars
falling from its rafters, faking the night sky.

For My Mother, Who Didn't Provide a Forwarding Address
Maari Carter

Every two hick town has orphaned mailboxes:
bills, coupons, TV Guide subscriptions scattered

over the hot blind earth, so no one thought
to wander down the gravel to your house,

decaying among overgrown persimmons and witch alder—
close enough to notice frayed window screens

under your carport or grume smudges on their panes.
I open the door you didn't bother to lock, when you moved

to Memphis with the truck driver from Wisconsin,
which sends a Diet Coke can, its tab inside, clinking

into the dining room past dried dog shit and the leftover
dead: Abby, muzzle full of blowflies, intestinal fluids

seeped onto kitchen's cheap vinyl, maggots dragging
the beds of her sockets, teeth still rooted

to blood drained gums, green-boned ribs
sticking out from her gas cracked chest.

The other two, Chinese Cresteds, side by side,
one further along than the other, both bloated

and stiff with rigor, lying beside a heap
of empty Marlboro cartons and fast food wrappers.

Outside, dirt daubers buzz above the nest-ridden concrete
and grandmother's Sweet Narcissus lean

against the porch. Belonging to you is a sucker punch,
and there is an us that won't go beyond today,

except when I feel you in my habits:
when the coffee strainer grows green mold

in my maker, cigarette filters slosh
at the bottoms of months old bottles, and dead fruit flies

confetti my refrigerator— or when I feel
some faint umbilical current, from a day tinted

with dogwood pollen; filled with grass juice smell,
when you held me steady on your shoulders, while I plucked

pears, hanging from the highest branches
and gathered them in the folds of your redwarm skirt.

Waffle House Rhapsody
Maari Carter

Before I was defibrillated
I was Miss Fairest of the Fair.

I heard my name over
the intercom and flounced

across the stockyard's sawdust
floor. You swivel

bare legged on a counter
stool, picking arm scabs

with scuzzy fingernails,
your carny-barker's biceps

twitching. I need you to love me
for my rib shears, when they remove

my crown with a skull key.
The waitress sulks

to freshen our coffee, her eyes
severe as an autopsy

report. You haven't touched
your omelet. I don't know why

we're here. Someone
has to sweep up your flesh

litter, rearrange my tweaked-out efforts
to color-code the sugar caddies.

I woke with corrosives
swirling my mouth, heart

monitor beeping like a garbage
truck. A nurse checked

vitals, dead ended her charts.
Blood spiraled the siphon

tube, and she said
I had gorgeous veins.

Tips
Lis Anna

Tupelo Honey's real mom died when she was real small but she loved her. That's how she ended up in the sticks with Auntie Monster and her boyfriend, Thursgood. It was funny how someone named him Thursgood, like he worked in Washington or was a King, because mostly he was good for nothing. At home it was all crazy, all the time. Auntie Monster called herself a business owner but they weren't nothing but a bunch of hooch runners. Hauling it. Drinking it. And whatever small amount of sane left in their brains was distilled a long time ago. But that place had a roof and walls. Or so they liked to remind her. Auntie and Thursgood had run off in the middle of the night in a frenzy of screaming and door slamming. The silence was nice but the shack was low on provisions.

Tupelo Honey put on her Sunday shirt and set off down the old, dirt path that led to the county line, and that's how she found that dead man floating face up, staring straight into the blazing gates of heaven. She'd never seen anything dead in all her life except maybe a bug or some furry thing squashed on the side of the road. The dead man's eyes bulged like the nastiest sight you done laid eyes on. But here's the thing. He was so quiet out there, floating under a clear, blue Mississippi morning with all of those Jesus bugs racing past his head. There had probably never been a finer morning in Jackson County and he was too dead to see it and Tupelo Honey thought that was a real shame.

She stared at him, trying to figure out if she'd ever seen him before and got this terrible fear he might step out of the water and snatch her up. She was gonna run away from the floating dead man when her eyes, god help her, caught a glimpse of those shiny new wing tips on his feet and boy were they nice. All leather and polished and pointy toed, looking like they cost a pretty penny. So, her mind got to thinking about how if she could get those shoes she could take them and sell them for money. And that was a fine plan so she rolled up her good pants and stepped barefoot out into the water where mud squished up between her toes. She said a quick prayer in Jesus' name cause she was about to lift some shoes off a dead man and would need a nod from the Holy Ghost. She reached down sure as she pleased and tugged a wet shoelace. The shoe was stiff and wet and she wrestled with it. The man kicked up a stink. She tugged hard. His body sloshed around in the water until the shoe came free and she tossed it onto the bank behind her. She leaned over again and tugged on the second one cause one shoe is useless unless it's a piece of art or something.

After she wrestled those shoes loose she took them over to the quiet, little boy in the house with the blue door off the boulevard. Then she walked right down to the police station and asked the woman with big hair and pink fingernails if she could talk to Sheriff Dietrich. He saw her right off, but wasn't smiling, because policemen are trained not to smile.

"Sheriff, there's a problem," she said.

That didn't make him look any happier. "What's going on, Tupelo Honey?"

"See I was walking down that old path that cuts from our property down to the county line and there's a dead man floating out on that lake where the Canadian geese come to hang out in the winter."

The Sheriff blinked. "What did you say?"

She sighed big and long and irritated and repeated what she'd just said.

"Are you saying you saw a dead body?"

"Yes, sir. Dead as you ever saw."

"Are you sure?" He knelt down and leaned in so close she could smell the bologna sandwich on his breath. "You're positive it wasn't just someone playing a prank?"

She thought about wrestling them shoes off of his big feet, knowing he was already up at the pearly gates with St. Peter trying to decide if he'd been naughty or nice and just kept that part to herself.

"He's floating out in the water, all bloated, staring straight up into the sun like it ain't burning holes through his eyeballs."

Sheriff put his hand on her shoulder and looked worried. "If you're telling the truth then I'll have to ride out with a deputy, and if we get out there and there's nothing going on then you'll cost the taxpayers a lot of money."

"I would never steal from a taxpayer," she said real loud.

Sheriff stood up and said to the big woman, "Get Officer Harper in here. We're going to ride out and see what Tupelo Honey is talking about." He adjusted his gun belt and turned to her. "You can ride in the patrol car."

She got to feeling all silly with excitement over riding in a real police car. The Sheriff let her ride in the middle and she pointed this way and that as Enoch Harper asked her questions and wrote the answers down in his little note pad. The Sheriff had no idea there was a bootlegger path back there and Tupelo Honey was kinda irked about having to reveal her secret pass through.

◆

Aesop was a quiet boy. He liked flowers, gardenias and braiding his mother's hair. That was before the war, before his daddy went off that fine day in June and returned in a box. He remembered his mother out on the front porch; hand over her mouth, talking to those men who'd come to tell her the truth. The locusts buzzed in anticipation of evening and the cicadas chirped. The sight of his mother crying, which he'd never seen before made him want to mash up all of the bad things in the world until they were nothing but a fine dust that he'd blow away like he blew out the candles on his ninth birthday. Daddy never saw his tenth. Aesop was a quiet

15

boy. He liked candy wafers and the women on Sunday all dressed for church. It was early summer and the earth was moist with the yielding plenty that came after a wet spring. You couldn't sit on the ground on account of the fact that a dark stain would appear on your britches so he sat out in the patio chairs rocking, watching his mother inside. She didn't cry anymore but she stared out the kitchen window at the carriage house where Daddy's workshop was set up. Nothing had been moved. Not a wrench or pipe or *Saturday Evening Post*. That's just the way it was.

Until that day in July when bugs were singing and his mother was in the kitchen cleaning pots and pans with bleach and the stinging in his nostrils was so awful that he walked out onto the front porch and watched the robins all a flitter in the birdbath. That odd little girl with the braids and buckteeth showed up, sneaking along the hedges. She asked him to keep an eye on a pair of shoes. Aesop was a quiet boy. The kind who could watch a pair of shoes and keep a secret for a long time. No one asked much of him. That crazy, little girl was like a crack of lightning in his life and made him smile. No one paid her any attention because her mama was dead and she lived out in the woods with a bunch of derelicts. He'd heard people around town talk about her when he was supposed to be buying flour for his mother. "That poor little girl," they'd say. And he'd stop listening and imagine the rest. That was his favorite part. Filling in all of the blank spaces with more interesting things. Like that pair of shoes, damp and musty, that sat on the windowsill in his bedroom under the blazing sunlight. Little flecks of dust rose in streams of light like a thousand tiny angels hovering to get a better look. Praise be to God, his mother would say.

He imagined that maybe those shoes were his daddy's and the little bucktooth girl found them in what could only be explained as a divine act of mystery. He took them gently from the windowsill, setting them quietly on the hard wood floor. He slipped his foot inside where it was cold and made his sock wet. His mother had cleaned his room for the day, so she'd be downstairs polishing and scrubbing and wouldn't bother him. He pulled off his wet sock, then the dry one and hid them both in the bottom of the clothes hamper, under the cloth used to wash behind his ears. Back at the windowsill he lifted the shoes again. The smell of lake soaked down into the soles, a smell so rich and black it spread out under everything, like the boogeyman, dark and unknowable.

Aesop was a quiet boy and lived up to this notion as he stepped barefoot into the shoes, first left, then right, riding back on his heels, just enough to lift the toes off of the floor. He imagined the sound of his daddy's footsteps on the stairs, calling out to his mother in a glorious roar, "I'm home, Sylvia. Where's my boy?" He imagined the very act of finding the shoes would draw his father back from the hereafter. It was then and there, Aesop knew he must hide them and never let them go.

◆

Lara had known sorrow. It wasn't a bother to her. The world went on spinning. A big, dusty, round rock that hurled through outer space. It was something she thought about often. Outer space. Two of the most boring words in the entire human language spoke separately but once combined they became exotic, the stuff of mystery.

Outer space.

Most of the space in her present world was filled with the long dead furniture of Mr. Morris' deceased mother, god rest her soul. A wife was not in his destiny, he said, what with all of the work he did and getting up in the middle of the night and having to go out because the world had come undone. Mr. Morris said respectable women couldn't live under the same roof once they knew what he'd seen. Lara hated the women who drowned their babies upside down in buckets of dirty water and the men who stabbed people until all of the blood ran out of their bodies and left them in the morgue. Mr. Morris had seen those things with his own eyes. That was why the Jim Beam bottle followed him from room to room. The bottle and Lara.

She reckoned she could wait a lifetime for a man like Mr. Morris to notice the pretty green flecks in her eyes and the way her white skin glowed all pretty in the late afternoon light. She wasn't an old maid yet. There was still time. So much of it. Time was another thing she considered on those mornings full of work. She imagined whole lives they'd never had together while she ironed his shirts, running her fingertips down the sleeves, lightly caressing the buttons, folding open the collars, unzipping the trousers. The bathroom smelled like shaving soap and Bay Rum. She inhaled deeply, polishing the faucets. The places she wanted to visit cascaded through her mind. The seven wonders of the world. They could see them together, hand in hand. Since her mama passed through the pearly gates no one waited on her to return home. They had been a small family. Then her mother fell down and Mr. Morris helped in every way, even carried her from the car into the house when she was discharged from the hospital. The whole time Lara stared up into the night sky trying to remember names of the constellations. Then Mr. Morris called her name and the sound of his voice was like a beacon in the darkest night and she followed.

Now his birthday had come around. In the old days his mother fussed and fiddled, putting a small party together for her only son. She bought a nicely decorated triple layer chocolate cake from the bakery and sent out invitations. It was nice. She was a good mother. But when she was gone, Lara realized that no one would be there to celebrate the day he was born. So, she made a secret trip downtown, wearing her navy coat and smart handbag. She wondered what in the world to buy until her eyes caught a glimpse of the perfect gift. A pair of Wing Tips sat on top of a display stand in the shoe department. A man needed a good pair of shoes. Sturdy, solid and attractive. A man needed a good pair of shoes to walk confidently into his future. She purchased the Tips on the spot and had the box wrapped in powder blue paper with a big silver bow.

◆

On his way into work, Detective Morris drove past the house on the boulevard with the blue door but didn't stop. Some nights he parked his unmarked Ford ten blocks down behind Jackson Tire and from there walked the distance through shrubs and silence to Sylvia's back porch. She, too, waited in the shadows and when she saw him they slipped quietly into the carriage house. In the dim light of the hurricane lamp her skin glowed the color of warm cinnamon. And his breath inhaled her kisses that landed on his lips and face and hands. Years passed in secret. Except before it was more complicated. Her husband had been alive, his mother, too. But the two obstacles to their future died away and he snuck over often to see her. If anyone recognized him prowling around in the shadows, he said he was on official police business. Even that would be different soon. They were going to move. All of them. Together. To the edge of Harlem where worlds converged and people didn't stare at the color of their skin and pinch the corners of their eyes up in disapproval. He had to think of the boy and his future. His boy. That strange, quiet boy who looked so much like him but with dark skin. He'd tried not to love her, for her sake, but he'd been terrible at not loving Sylvia. Be careful who you love because you'll love them forever, his mother used to say. Truer words were never spoken. From the first time he'd seen Sylvia walking home from church when he was just seventeen, he'd loved her madly. Now she was a widow. And once you've married the wrong person and been set free you look upon the world with a bigger vision, a little hunger, that rumbles deep in your belly.

 He looked down at the pot roast sandwich Lara packed in his lunch. The reports on his desk sat in a golden pool of lamplight. The station was quiet. At that hour most desks were empty. His eyes drifted to the stack of reports. He'd spent all day running leads and come up with zero. The big black rotary phone on his desk rang. The metal spring on his chair groaned as he rolled forward to answer.

 "Jackson County Sheriff's Department. Detective Morris speaking."

 "What's buzzin, cuzzin?"

 "Who is this?"

 "Is this the heat?"

 Detective Morris straightened in his seat. "Who is this?"

 "Who I am doesn't matter jive daddy. Who I know is what makes a difference."

 "Who do you know?"

 "You know how you're always looking for those hooch runners filling up your county with Shine?"

 "How do you know that?"

 "Because I've seen you out there hoofing it in Nowheresville, man. Listen. You got something I want. I got something you want."

 "What's that?"

 "Tips."

 "Tips?"

 "Yeah, like where those hillbilly hooch runners are and how they're sneaking it down an old, dirt path straight to the county line. Your county line."

"How do you know?"

"Same way I know the sky is blue. I seen it."

Detective Morris shuffled papers around on his desk looking for something to write with. Finally, he flipped the top of his fountain pen off. "Give me directions. I'll drive over check it out."

The moon glowed high in the sky. Detective Morris pulled his unmarked Ford into a grove of trees, cut the engine and listened. Tree frogs and locusts hummed. Insects chirped skeet skeet skeet. The earth was soft. He looked down at his new wing tips. It was the first time he'd thought of anything other than busting up a Moon shine ring in the half an hour it took him to drive out to the woods, based on a tip from a slick mouth stranger trying to bust his cousin out of county jail.

Light from the dashboard reflected off his shiny wing tips. A more practical man would have the sense to keep a spare set of shoes in the trunk. Barefoot was not an option. Hell, if he ruined them, he'd drive down to the department store and buy a new pair, so as not to hurt Lara's feelings. His eyes adjusted to the dark silhouette of leaves under the light of a full moon. He closed the door to the Ford gently, certain he knew how to cut down the path by the lake without getting lost. The slick mouthed stranger delivered detailed instructions during the call. He was hot to get his cousin out. Morris was hot to bust up a Shine ring and get the letter of recommendation needed to transfer to a precinct in Harlem. He passed the lake with the tree frogs covering up the sound of his footsteps with their loud, ancient song. He was sure he'd walked more than a mile when a lamplight flickered in the distance. He slowed to a stop, his ears trying to discern each sound. Footsteps, bottles clanking, car doors opening and closing. He pressed forward, to the edge of the wood, where he saw plain as day, a lamp in the window of an old shack. He patted his hip several times before realizing in his haste he'd left his gun belt back at the station, hanging on his chair. He bent over to pull his backup .38 Special from a leg holster when he heard a single twig snap. Morris rose up fast, flashed his badge. The dark figure of a man watched.

The wind blew through the trees, and a whip-poor-will broke into its haunting song. Then the hard blow of a pipe wrecked his brain. He stumbled, turned, and was smacked again harder. His nose burned, blood filled his mouth. He fell to the ground, and reached for his holster but heard the crack of his own skull and felt the pain rush down his arm in a thunderous rage. By now he realized there was more than one dark figure. He tried to tell them he was on official police business, to put his hands in the air, but the words mixed with blood in his throat and gurgled, until he sputtered and closed his eyes. An image of Sylvia filled his mind. He could see her standing, bright and pretty in a white dress with tiny blue birds flying around the hem. The rich, brown of her skin glowed copper in the fading sunlight. She held out her hand to him as she called to their son. But he could not reach her and his eyes drifted to the lightning bugs, hovering and flickering above the lush mid summer grass. He felt a dark stranger pull his gun from the holster, then drag him along the path. Rocks dug into his shoulder blades but he could not move. Some deep, hidden fear in him rose up. Off in the distance he heard the sound of a little girl singing and he begged with all his strength, please find my boy. Tell him I'm coming home.

Illustration by Stephen Smith

Light on Rust
Tobi Cogswell

Greenwood, Mississippi

Burned trees, standing water.
Snow-blind and still, plowed
rows conjure rice paddies.
The sky exhales.

Another time, green is green,
now tar-paper roofs sag,
a finger-snap between lightning
and thunder – explosives
in the war zone between
low-pressure and river.

Restless birds warned of this,
took refuge in the eaves
of boarded-up churches
and empty, moss-covered
used up homes.
Come spring, they find us.

Tired, Can't Sleep, Want Drink, Need Hug
Tobi Cogswell

That sadness of the spirit—
the clock marches a soldierly horror show
and brown is desert wrapped with low.
Chain-gang of weariness and blues,
everyone gets this way sometimes.

Two dead crows on the lawn today
an old apple core untouched,
the buzzing sound of anyone's
small plane and no one knows
why anything happens.

Mostly just an ordinary summer
but music is missing and clouds keep
the sun from burning a hole in the sky.
Bitter on the lips, smile rhymes
with hypocrite.

The kindness of touch,
burn of a shot of gold.
Eyes that stare into the night,
too hot to sleep, too lonely
to make love how long…

how long

At Altitude
Tobi Cogswell

Jackson, Mississippi

Her skin was the color
of an Indian summer
on the Sunflower River
with light full blazing.

She had two babies, tall
as roadside blossoms,
one in a dress yellow
as field daisies, the other
in the rusted color
of old rail spikes.

She kept them neat and quiet,
but when hungry they could
howl up the dead with a witches
broom of screams.

Her husband had the bottles –
he and his honeysuckle vodka
gone, vanished in an airplane even
skinny folk couldn't hide in.

No one looked at her, mostly
stared at her girls, bright
as summers on the Natchez Trace,
mean-willed as weather.

I took one baby, bounced her
as she played with my glasses.
My man took the other.
Our new woman friend,
beaten with shame and humbled
with anger, patted our shoulders,
went searching for milk.

We knew she'd be back,
kissed each other over the tops
of those sweet babies heads,
wished we could keep them
just a little bit longer, however
long that was gonna be,
just a little bit longer.

Abalone
Tobi Cogswell

The perfect pearl
thick with platinum and shined
with dignity and respect.
Smell of wax, cut grass,
and nostalgia
like the days of barber poles,
white gloves and library cards,
beekeepers and family dinners.

A sweet wide seat for sitting close,
radio that plays only blues and bible -
close your eyes at the railroad crossing,
listen for the gate to go up,
you are in a town checkerboarded
with roads and not much else.

You wear white t-shirts,
she wears heels.
You have a flask,
she has lipstick, and the filmiest
scarf - she looks like Sophia Loren
in some movie you can't see
at the drive-in anymore.
You call her doll, she blushes.

A windshield wide as a wharf,
thick white sidewalls, and a wish
not everyone has the hunger
to make come true. Fingertips
grazing on that smooth shine
grandly waken a concerto for one.

How Jo-Beth Came to Love the Sky
Tobi Cogswell

Clouds are the lecture hall of God.
High cirrus wisps are tears of women
walking the Widow's Walk, waiting
for their men to come home from sea.
Cumulus are the beefy bullies
in the football uniforms of the universe.
If they had sound, and sometimes they do,
they would be the drumline announcing
their arrival, daring anyone not to notice.
The broom of wind, sweeping dust
off the hearth of heaven, sometimes
a promenade of sociability and others
a run for cover. And always the birds,
riding the highs and lows, gliders over
invisible peaks caused by air, the hidden
sea, from below. Birds don't take a weather
class, they just know. Gray or any shade
turning toward dawn or blue, she would
lie on the grass, red-velvet-cake blanket
wrapped around her for warmth. She would
climb into the stories of the sky. From squirrels
jumping from roof to tree, to a web shining
with droplets of dew, to the helicopter
heard but not seen until long past overhead,
destination unknown and wide-eyed.
There's a lot you can imagine.

Resurrection Fern
CL Bledsoe

The day Joey turned thirteen, which happened to be a Saturday, he got up to eat cereal just like any other day. His sister, Chyna, came down and got a bowl, and they sat at the table and ate.

"Where's mom?" Joey asked.

Chyna shrugged and answered noncommittally. "Why?" she asked as an afterthought.

"Just wondering," Joey answered. He dropped his spoon into the bowl with a gloop.

His sister's hairspray smelled like electric rain – her hair was frozen into a stiff approximation of life, all curly and big. Her face was hidden beneath a layer of makeup that resembled colored flour. She smelled like cigarettes and a perfume he couldn't name, not that it would matter if he could.

"Where you going?" He asked her.

"Jonesboro," she said. "With the girls."

He didn't answer. "Hey, what's today's date?" He tried.

"Fuck if I know," she said. He nodded and got up to rinse out his bowl. "You going to take a shower or anything?"

"I already did," he said.

"Come on and go to town with me," she said.

"I think I'm going to just stick around here in case mom needs me."

She frowned at him. "Mom doesn't need anything. Come on."

He mumbled an argument, but she ignored him and headed out the door. When he didn't follow, she honked, making him look back towards his mom's and Tommy's, her boyfriend, door in fear. She honked again, and he heard a noise from their room and ran out to her.

"Where are we going?" Joey asked. The car was filling up, and he was feeling pretty sorry for himself. He was in the back, squeezed between two hefty girl friends of Chyna's whose names he could never remember. He thought of them as Thing 1 and Thing 2. A little blonde thing named Sara was up front. She frightened him a little.

"The getting place," Sara said.

They pulled up to a liquor store, and the girls filed out. Joey tried to stay, but Chyna leaned in and looked at him. "Get out," she said.

"I'll just wait."

"Get out."

"But..."

She reached in and grabbed his shirt and yanked him to the car door.

"Fine," he said.

Inside, the girls spread out in ones or twos, making jokes and pointing and laughing. Chyna led Joey to the counter.

"Hey Keith," she said to the guy working there. "Long shift?"

His whole face spread into a smile. "Yeah, you know." He kept nodding but Joey couldn't tell what for.

"This is my brother, Joey. It's his birthday."

Joey's head whipped around to look at her, but she was looking at Keith.

"Cool, cool," Keith said, nodding. "Happy birthday, little man."

"When do you get off?" Sara asked.

"Four," Keith said, nodding. "What are you doing?"

"We might swing by."

"Cool." Keith nodded.

"All right." Sara smiled.

Chyna headed back deeper into the store, with Joey following. "Okay," she said. "What do you want?" Joey gave her a blank stare. "For your birthday."

"Um," Joey said.

Thing 2 appeared and leaned in to him "We're going to get you fucked up."

"What?" Joey said.

"You want tequila?" Chyna held up a bottle.

"Si, senor," Thing 2 said in a bad Spanish accent.

"I don't know," Joey said. "What about cake?"

"They don't have cake, here," Chyna said. "So pick one."

"He don't know what he wants," Sara said.

Joey looked at some of the bottles; they all looked very similar. He didn't really know much about alcohol, and he hadn't really been thinking about drinking.

"What does mom drink?" he asked.

"Rum. Ugh," Chyna said.

He walked down the aisle a little and found one that looked interesting and held it up for Chyna.

"Margarita mix?"

He shrugged and started to put it back.

"We need salt," Thing 2 said, coming up behind him. She grabbed the bottle. Joey glanced at Chyna who was holding the tequila bottle.

"Triple Sec," Thing 1 said.

Joey had no idea what they were talking about. They gathered ingredients and took them to the counter, waiting until there weren't any other customers to do so.

Keith rang them up, no longer nodding, but instead glancing to the door every few seconds.

"You guys get caught," he said. "Tell—"

"Tell them you traded us booze for sexual favors?" Sara said.

Keith grinned.

"We'll be cool," Chyna said. "We won't get caught, and if we do, we'll say we got it from our parents."

"Cool." Keith nodded again.

He rang them up and gave them the bag.

"Hey, what time do you get off?" Sara asked.

Keith got a pained expression. "Four."

"Yeah. Cool," Sara said. "Maybe we'll swing by."

He didn't look convinced as they left, giggling, and Sara called out, "Not!"

They went to Sara's trailer to mix the drinks. Her mom was home, but didn't care what they did as long as they didn't bother her while she watched TV. Things 1 & 2 mixed it and poured it in mason jars and put salt all along the lips and handed one to Joey. He wiped away some of the salt to take a drink, and Sara smacked him in the back of the head.

"The salt's part of it," she said in response to Chyna's glare.

"I know." He blushed. "I just wanted to try it without."

He sipped and tasted a little bit of salt. The drink was good. Fruity. He took another big swallow.

The girls were giggling, talking about Keith and other people from school. After he finished the glass, the girls made him another one. Joey was feeling good, better than he'd felt that morning when he thought no one would remember his birthday.

"We should get some pot," Thing 2 said.

"I can't drive, though," Sara said. "My mom doesn't want me driving on my own with just a permit."

"I'll drive," Chyna said. "My mom doesn't care."

They turned off the main drag of town – Highway 1 – into the parking lot of a strip mall Joey didn't think he'd ever been in before. It had a bunch of stores with names he didn't recognize. He assumed if he didn't know the name of a store in a strip mall it probably sold women's clothes.

Joey felt like he was floating in a beautiful sea of greeny/yellow goodness. He felt totally at ease and closed his eyes. On either side of him, Thing 1 and Thing 2 were mashed against him. They kept moving: leaning up to talk to Sara or Chyna. Their motions rocked him like the movement of water. They both smelled good, too, like girls: makeup and hairspray and perfume.

They pulled up next to another car, and Chyna was talking to the driver. Sara kept leaning over and yelling things in her garish, redneck voice. Joey kept his eyes closed.

"How you feeling there, Joey?" Thing 2 asked.

"Good. How are you?"

She giggled and he felt motion as she moved her hand on his leg. Suddenly, pinpricks erupted along his leg and stomach. The hand crept up his knee to his thigh. Thing 2 leaned in to his ear and whispered something Joey didn't actually hear, but the thrill of her breath on his ear was the best thing he'd ever felt.

"What?" he whispered back.

"Do you like me?" Thing 2 asked.

"Sure," he said, liking her a lot better in the last few minutes. "I like you."

She slid her hand up to his crotch and squeezed what she found there. He waited for her to do more, but she was suddenly involved in the conversation with whoever was in the other car.

Joey was annoyed; his state of joyful flotsam had been shattered. The car beside them revved and jerked forward. The girls were haggling, that much he could tell. The other car jerked forward again and something flew in and hit Joey in the face. It was a Ziploc bag. He didn't think about it, just grabbed it and threw it back, hitting the driver of the other car in the back of the head as he drove off. Bastard, Joey thought.

Chyna eased the car forward. "Where is it?" she asked.

Thing 1 and Thing 2 searched the floorboards and backseat while Joey tried to regain his zen-like state from earlier.

"We can't find it!" Thing 2 said.

"Is Joey sitting on it?" Chyna asked. She pulled over, and they all got out. Thing 2 had to drag Joey out.

"It's not here," Thing 2 said.

"Joey?" Chyna asked.

"What?" He opened his eyes. It was bright out. They were standing in the Hardees parking lot. Sara advanced on him and grabbed his shirt.

"Where's the weed?"

"Huh?" Joey thought. "Ah."

"Ah?" Chyna asked.

Sara grabbed his nipple and twisted it. "Where's the weed?" she repeated.

"I didn't know," he said. "It hit me in the face, so..."

"So?" Chyna said.

"So I threw it back."

Sara slapped him in the head again. The two Things looked like they wanted to kill him.

"We've got to catch Barry," Chyna said.

"We should leave dumbass here," Sara said.

"He's drunk," Chyna said. "He doesn't know what he's doing."

Barry laughed a lot about it, but Joey liked him because he seemed to like Joey.

"You don't take no shit, huh?" he said.

Joey shrugged. Barry acted like he was going to make them pay for it again until Sara promised to blow him. "I don't want your skanchy mouth on me," he said.

Sara sulked after that, and after Barry gave them the baggie and took off again, she turned around and punched Joey hard in the stomach.

"What the fuck, bitch?" he sputtered.

The two Things held him back and Sara reared up in the front seat. "Bitch? Who you calling bitch you little faggot?"

"Sit the fuck down, Sara," Chyna said.

"That little shit called me a bitch," she said, her voice indignant.

"Sit the fuck down, bitch!" Chyna said.

"Not a bitch," Sara said, her voice whiny, now. She slumped in the front seat. Joey coughed in the backseat, his feeling of serenity totally gone.

Chyna headed out to Summersweet and the network of gravel roads that intersected it South of town, around the state park. Thing 1 rolled a joint and lit it and passed it up to Chyna who passed it to Sara and then Thing 2 who started to hand it to Joey.

"Oh hell no," Sara said. "You're not giving that him."

"Why not?" Thing 2 said.

"He didn't put in on it."

"I put it on it," Chyna said.

"I don't want his mouth on it," Sara said.

"I don't want anything your skanchy mouth has been on," Joey said.

"I got this," Thing 2 said. "Shotgun." She took a hit, leaned in to Joey, and blew a long train into his open mouth. "Hold it in," she said. He held the smoke, searching her eyes, which were soft and joyful. He coughed, suddenly, and she passed the joint around to Thing 1.

The next time it came around, Thing 2 brushed her lips against Joey's when she exhaled into his mouth. He didn't cough, even though he wanted to. The third time, he started to feel himself sink back into the water. They finished the joint and Sara swallowed it. Chyna turned the music on, and all of them chattered over the top of it. Thing 2's hand was on Joey's leg. He was pretty sure he was in love.

They came into town to hit a gas station and use the bathroom. There was a line for the girls, but Joey went right in. The door burst open as he was peeing, and Sara strode in. Joey froze mid-stream.

"Screw that," she said. "I ain't waiting." She went over to the toilet. "Did you piss on this thing?" Joey concentrated on finishing and didn't answer. He stared straight ahead. There was a machine on the wall that sold condoms and other things. There were pictures that looked exotic and a little confusing to Joey.

"There's a condom machine," Joey said.

"Don't get any ideas," Sara said from right beside him. He jumped a little. She was staring at his penis. He put it away. "Not bad," she said, a little impressed. Joey blushed sunburn red, and she started laughing.

Sara left but Joey stayed behind to wash his hands. The door opened again, and he ignored it until he felt a body pressed into his, breasts in his back, hands reaching around to his stomach. He shivered.

"Sara?" he said.

"No, idiot," Thing 2 said. She pushed him into the sink.

"Oh, sorry. She was in here…" He turned around and saw the girl's angry face. "I was freaking out."

She relaxed a little. The awkwardness weighed on Joey. He stepped to her and kissed her. She let him. He felt like a fish just standing there, so he moved his hands over her body. She opened her blouse and let him kiss her chest. She uncapped her breasts, and he kissed her nipples. Her hand was on him and undid his pants. She wrapped her fingers around him, squatted down and took him in her mouth, and he was finished. She coughed, surprised, and laughed. He blushed again, and she kept working him. He stayed hard, and this time, it took longer. When it was over, she stood back up with a smile, and he said,

"I love you," even though he still wasn't sure what her name was.

She laughed, and said, "Happy Birthday." And kissed him on the cheek.

When they got back out to the car, the girls all burst out laughing. Sara looked at him and he knew she'd told them something. In the backseat, Thing 2 didn't put her hand on his leg again. He wasn't sure what that meant, so he let it go.

◆

After she dropped the girls off, Chyna pulled up to Hays Food Town. Joey started to get out, but she said, "Stay in the car." She hopped out, left the car running and the door open, and ran up to the sidewalk. There were ferns and potted plants and no one was around. She grabbed one and ran back to the car and handed it to him.

"Happy Birthday," she said. "You like ferns, right?" she added as an afterthought.

"Yeah," he said, though he'd never considered it before.

"Cool." She turned on the radio. It was Van Halen, "Jump." "Sellout bullshit," she said and turned the station. They didn't find anything worth listening to all the way home, so they just listened to the sound of the car as it cut through the wind.

Tongue Economics
John Davis, Jr

Danny Tillman eats [MF]ing mayflies for a quarter.
He waggles thin lips, [F]ing fake-chews, jaw bobbing,
then gulps as if [GD] dish soap tastes better.
His minister father believes in Palmolive
punishment: purifier, reminder, spirit-cure
for boys who take the Lord's name in vain, curse.
A little green dab on tainted taste buds cleanses
sin and sugar-stained palates, color-coated
by twenty-five-cent machines' bubble gum – forbidden
sweet chasers to purge, forgive and forget flavors:
[SOB] bugs and betrayals for silver.

Echoes and Starch
Justin Brouckaert

I.

Carrie is an awful cook.

Victor and I watched her fumble with stovetop dials from the safety of the kitchen table, cradling cups of black coffee and providing play-by-play for her culinary failures.

"Carrie," Victor said. "You're a terrible cook."

She glaced back at us and feigned anger before scraping the burnt remains of pasta fagioli that looked like caviar onto our plates.

"Carrie," Victor said. "That looks like caviar."

"Well, it's pasta fagioli," she replied, sprinkling Parmesan cheese over the meal.

Summers in North Carolina are relentless, and we didn't help matters by spending most of our time crammed into one room, a cupboard-sized kitchen with just enough space for an oven, a refrigerator and a shaky half-moon table Victor paid 5 dollars for at a garage sale. The place heated up fast when we all started talking, but Victor and I thrived on routine: For us, six o'clock meant a fresh pot of coffee and watching Carrie struggle through another new recipe. The three of us had been living together for more than four years, and cooking was the one chore Carrie had agreed to. Unfortunately for Victor and me, it just happened to be the one she was worst at.

"I'm not going to be your mother, you know," she had told me when she first settled into our second-floor apartment, peppering our bare walls with photo collages and framed prints of sunsets on water. She was still shaky from the move, mostly from the rifts it had made between her and her family.

"Well, don't be my mother, then," I told her. "And don't be your mother, either."

These things are often harder than they sound.

Carrie's mother was nothing short of saintly, a pious old woman whose idea of a good time was to cook three full meals for her family every day. She was president of her church's ladies guild nine years running and a Sunday school teacher since the age of 17 – the type of woman whose hair looked better gray.

It wasn't her piety that made me dislike her; I had no problem with religion. I had no problem with Carrie's mother, either, but it's tough to salvage a relationship with someone who blames you for the corruption of her daughter's soul. She had fought our relationship to the messy end, jamming her stubby body in the doorframe to block Carrie from retrieving the last of her things. Her father's response was simpler: If she left, it would be for good.

Before Carrie, Victor and I had always taken turns washing dishes, taking out the trash, mopping the floors. There was an old AM/FM radio on the kitchen counter that we would turn full volume whenever it was time to clean. I listened to classic rock: Aerosmith, Def Leppard, Guns 'n' Roses. I sang along with Steven and Eddie, playing air guitar with oven pans. Victor listened to classical music, and washed the dishes on his toes.

After Carrie moved in, it took her all of a week to get antsy.

"John, let me do *something*," she sighed when she finally gave in, watching Victor squeeze half our last bottle of dish soap on a greasy pan.

"What do you mean, do something? Do whatever you want," I told her, flopping onto a chair with a newspaper.

"No, I mean something for you two."

"I thought you weren't going to be our mother."

She watched Victor miss the surface of the pan and punch straight into the sink, drenching himself with soap water and soggy chicken nugget bits. He turned to us and blinked.

"Well, maybe you could use a mother or two." She paused for a moment, touching a fingernail to her chin.

"I've got it!" she said. "I'll cook for you."

"Carrie, it's fine," I said, glancing over at Victor. "We've been cooking our own meals for years."

"Oh, when have you ever cooked a *meal?*"

In the kitchen, Victor was stripping free of his T-shirt. I watched his ribs shift as he wrung the shirt into the sink.

Victor had been thin for as long as I'd known him. We didn't have a lot to spend on food, but that didn't seem to have much to do with it; mostly, Victor just wasn't that interested in eating. He found what he liked in frozen mini-pizzas, peanut butter sandwiches, and fast food dollar menus, and he stuck with it.

"That's what I'll do," she said. "I'll cook for you."

Victor wailed with Mozart in the kitchen.

Carrie began looking after us in other ways, too, always when we least expected it. Victor and I would do laundry together and leave the dry clothes in baskets near the TV; it was our weekly ritual to watch sports and fold clothes together, but occasionally we'd walk in from a game of pick-up ball to find them already folded.

"Carrie," Victor said when he caught her. "These aren't your clothes."

"They're your clothes, Vic!" she said, smiling. She placed the last neatly folded shirt on top of the pile and offered him the basket.

He leaned over and petted her gently on the head.

"It's a wonderful thing you've done here, darling."

She laughed and swatted his hand away.

"Vic, they're just T-shirts!"

But he was already gone, waltzing away with the laundry basket, humming Tchaikovsky under his breath.

II.

Whenever we had some money, Carrie and I would wait for Victor to get home from working at the factory, and the three of us would walk down to Duke's Bar so Victor could play the jukebox. Duke's was almost always empty, but Victor would put on an old country song and make partners with the first woman he found.

"Darling," he said in his best drawling Russian accent, to a hulking 30-year old woman in a cut-off denim vest and mud-spattered boots. Forty years old in leather and chains. Nearing fifty in a track jacket and loafers. "Darling, you are beautiful. Dance with me."

Carrie and I swayed together near the bar and watched a 200-pound Hank Williams, Jr. fanatic swing Victor around the dance floor like a blanket in the wind. He whinnied with glee and winked at us through a matted clump of hair as he flew past, and when the dance ended, he gave each woman a kiss square on the nose.

"John, didja get a loada that one?" Victor said to me later at the bar, out of breath, handing the bartender another sweaty dollar bill.

"I sure did, Vic," I said, watching him grip a frosty bottleneck from the grinning woman behind the counter. He wheezed out a laugh, clapped me on the shoulder and gave Carrie a nudge on his way to find another.

At night, Carrie and I made love to the sound of cartoons and Victor crunching on Honeycomb in the next room over, hearing his laughter through the walls.

When I left the room to use the bathroom afterward, Victor greeted me in the hallway and grabbed me by the shoulders with both hands.

"Ya did good, kid," he said with a wink. "Ya did real good."

He gave me a kiss square on the nose and closed the bathroom door, leaving me in the hallway smelling milk and cereal.

III.

Victor had been working at the local plant outside of Greensboro ever since his father, my uncle, put him out at age 16. He was just a name to me then, and the news of big Victor kicking little Victor out of the house had passed to me through my mother, who would never speak of the incident in anything above a whisper. All I knew was that big Victor had a history of alcohol and a heavy hand, and little Victor had a history of not saying much about it. We didn't see either of them very often, and besides, I was only 14 and miles away, putting up 300 jump shots every night trying to make my school's freshman team.

After I had lived out my hoop dreams – graduating from N.C. State with six career minutes, two career points and a degree in general business – I moved to the city and got a job as a gas station cashier down the block from my apartment complex, the cheapest one in the Raleigh area.

I never had any interest in business. During college, studying had seemed like a waste of perfectly good time that could have been spent in the gym putting in hours that the second-string shooting guard was spending on algebra. I scraped through school spending most of my time in the gym or at the rec, but the extra practice didn't help. Whether I believed it or not, I was an undersized walk-on lucky to make the team to begin with.

After graduation I had an easy enough time finding a temporary job but a harder time putting my dreams to the side. I spent most of my time running half-court ball with community college dropouts, sometimes scoring all 11 points in games against guys that weren't good enough to hold a junior college roster spot. It was enough to justify my stubborn belief that I could have been a D1 starter, or at least enough to vent my frustration that I hadn't been.

I stayed out late to play ball every night, and it wasn't too long before I missed enough morning shifts to lose my job at the gas station. I had a lot more time to play ball after that, and that's what I did, watching my savings get siphoned into rent payments and cheap pizza in the meantime.

My mother called me one morning to tell me Victor had lost his apartment and might need a place to stay. Her argument was that we'd both been struggling with money, even though I insisted I could find some sort of job if I really needed to. It was years before I met Carrie, years before I had really even started to try.

"It wouldn't hurt to have someone help with rent," she reminded me. I cursed her logic under my breath.

"I don't need a roommate."

"I heard you need a roommate," Victor said, standing at my doorway two hours later with a torn nylon suitcase under one arm and a deflated basketball under the other.

I stared hard at the worn leather.

"You play?" I asked.

"I watch."

"U.N.C. or N.C. State?"

Victor turned his head and spit off my porch.

"Fuck Roy Williams."

I stared at him, his sweaty gray T-shirt. He was disheveled, unshaven and hopelessly goofy –a real-life cartoon character. I couldn't help but grin.

"Come on in, Victor."

"Thankee, cousin."

Victor and I didn't have a lot in common, but we both loved sports and fell into habits easily. For us, that was enough. He had a job at a nearby sports equipment factory that he worked at during the daytime while I slept in or held odd jobs. At night we ran the courts, walking the four blocks to the only park in the area where anyone played.

Victor didn't have much confidence in his game at first. The two of us would shoot around every night before the pick-up games started, sometimes running drills or playing H-O-R-S-E until the rest of the guys arrived. It wasn't much of a pick-up scene – most of the guys were rec-ball lifers from high school or community college: speedsters too trigger-happy around the 3-point line and too reckless under the rim after the JuCo circuit spit them out. They came around 8:30, and we would play until after midnight. There were 12 of us at most, and never anyone new.

I could take the ball to the rack against most of the guys we faced, but I liked running the offense through Victor. We had a handful of plays that the two of us ran by feel and plenty more that I had taught him, but usually we just relied on fundamentals, using the pick and roll or screens to set him free for easy buckets: layups, floaters, quick bank shots from the key. It was simple, and it worked.

Victor certainly didn't look like a basketball player. He was a lanky 6-foot-5 and sported long black hair that seemed to poof out rather than slick down when he sweated. He was a natural in the post no matter how much the other guy outweighed him, and he could pass the ball as well as he could shoot. He never shot the long ball, though. He always took a few steps in or kicked it around the arc instead – said it wasn't his job to shoot the three.

I would carry the ball up the court, dart around a high screen and then slide the ball to Victor in the paint. He wasn't strong, but he was slippery; he found ways to wrap himself around his defenders, slinking through them to the basket and finishing with layups that trickled all the way around the rim before dropping in.

His unorthodox style made him popular with the guys. He was the type of player they all wanted to give a nickname: *String Bean. Gangles. The Sapling.* They were impressed by his pliancy, the ways he could stretch and bend his arms through traffic around the rim. It was a mystery, they thought, how he moved the way he did.

Finally they decided that as far as names go, Victor was a silly enough one to fit his game.

It went like that, before Carrie came along, with Victor and I spending every free hour together: playing ball, debriefing the games on the walk back to the apartment, taunting each other in one of Victor's many accents, screaming at the television together whenever a game was on.

Usually we talked sports – how the Huskies were doing, what to make of their next freshman class, if they'd ever make another run like '83. Sometimes we stopped for a case of beer on our way back and stayed up long after Carrie went to sleep, *Cheers*-ing to SportsCenter Top 10 plays and mocking the news anchors. Our talks often turned to family on those nights – how my mother used to drive me across the state for travel basketball games, or how Victor's cousin was making $75,000 a year as a switchperson for Union Pacific – but any talk of Victor's father always ended abruptly.

"It's all just flies in the wind, Johnny. Flies in the wind," he'd say, and whistle a mournful dirge.

IV.

I was working part-time at a sandwich shop downtown when I first met Carrie. She was doing her student teaching at a nearby elementary school, so she came into the shop wearing polka-dot dresses and trying to flirt with me at the deli. She came in for lunch every day for nearly two months before I finally picked up on things and asked her out.

I never stepped back to analyze why a girl like Carrie would be interested in someone who couldn't even make a decent turkey & swiss. She and I just fit; her ambition kept me motivated, my humor kept her loose. Everybody won – except for her mother, who never laughed at my jokes and didn't know a damn thing about basketball. She never understood why her daughter couldn't find someone with a real job – someone taller, more Presbyterian.

I never asked Carrie to choose between her family and me, but she did it anyway.

Now she taught fifth grade at a city school while I spent most of my time looking for work, long removed from my stint at the sandwich shop. I never minded the job, but being with Carrie made me want to do something more meaningful than dealing pastrami on stale rye and rehashing gray hamburger meat into chili.

I scoured the city for anything that could classify as a real job, applying for grunt roles at banks, insurance companies, and even managerial slots in retail. The search was full-time: I hadn't had any jobs or internships in college, so I tried to catch up by spending hours at the library searching for interview tips, scouring the classifieds, researching the different companies where I was applying. Occasionally I spent a few weeks doing odd jobs and construction work under the table with an old college teammate, just to help with rent.

It would have been easy just to find part-time work, but Carrie's enthusiasm was contagious. For the first time, I really did believe it wouldn't be long before I snagged the big one – something I could see myself doing for more than just a year or two, something with salary and benefits and a company picnic, the whole package. Carrie cheered me on each step of the way, and her enthusiasm made me numb enough to accept that I was living off her in the meantime.

But the more her cheers clashed with real-world rejection, the more I began to feel like a leech.

Carrie wasn't necessarily an optimist; her idealism wasn't based on any fundamental belief that life would get better, but instead seemed a result of a complete commitment to her new family, to making everything work. Even in those early days she was desperate to make things perfect, trying to finish my sentences and failing.

"I just feel —"

"Tired?" We were settling into bed and ending a long discussion about my job search.

"Pathetic," I said.

"You're not pathetic," she said. "Not everyone finds a job right away."

"I'm just —"

"Unlucky?"

"Frustrated."

"Don't give up," she cooed. "I have enough money. I can pay your share of the rent too, for a while."

It was enough to make a man turn to crime.

By 5 o'clock I'd be defeated, holding my head in my hands at the kitchen table when Carrie came in to give me a hug and start dinner. Victor arrived home from the plant an hour later, giving me a kiss on the nose and starting a pot of coffee while he laughed at Carrie's homemade Alfredo sauce.

"Carrie," Victor said, "that looks like vanilla ice cream."

"Well, it's Alfredo sauce," she replied, mixing in bits of chicken that looked like beef jerky.

V.

Victor and I spent every Saturday afternoon folding laundry in the living room and watching college basketball on a 12-inch television Victor had to hit with a broomstick every five minutes to refocus. After he settled into his chair, he'd pour a bag of pistachios and a bag of sunflower seeds in a bowl together and pick it clean, even licking salt trails off the plastic. This, too, was ritual.

"Man, your cholesterol has to be through the roof," I told him one day, watching him clear half the bowl with a scoop of his hand.

He crunched noisily and blinked at me.

"Victor, I know you know what cholesterol is."

He grinned and smacked the television with the broomstick.

"At least I don't eat the shells," he said, "even though I heard they're good for you."

"They're good for cutting you up inside."

"That hurts, Johnny. You know, I'm as healthy as a bull."

"An ox, Victor. You're as healthy as an ox."

Victor beamed and thanked me for the compliment.

Whenever N.C. State played, we both sat on the edge of our chairs and yelled curses at every wild pass or clanging miss. Carrie smiled and shook her head, grading word problems in the kitchen.

"That's a terrible shot," I groaned.

"Carrie, did you see that shot?" Victor asked, slamming the broomstick to the floor.

"No, Vic, I must have missed it."

"She didn't see the shot, Victor," I said through my hands.

"How could she? She's not even watching the game!" Victor hands went wild when he was angry; he ran them through his hair faster than the tousled bloom could settle. "It was a terrible shot, darling, you can trust us for that."

"That should be me out there," I grumbled.

The worst part about failing as a college basketball player was that I hadn't even realized I'd been failing until the day I graduated. I got by with the little athletic talent I had by putting my head down and working hard – this, I'd been told, was all it took. The possibility of being a career bench player hadn't seemed like a reality until the buzzer sounded on our final game.

It took me a while to get over the hangover after basketball ended. For the longest time, I felt detached, distorted without the boundaries I had tried so hard to fit within. Even now it hurt to watch games on TV, but it was more of a dull ache than an actual pain, and living with Victor tended to make everything seem a little bit less serious.

"That should be you and me out there," Victor said, stuffing a handful of pistachios in his mouth.

"That should be us out there!" Carrie yelled from the kitchen.

Victor gave the television another smack with the broomstick, and I couldn't help but laugh.

VI.

I was drinking coffee at the kitchen table one morning when Victor walked into the apartment with a book. He opened the door slowly, poking his head through the crack and hiding it behind him, but when he saw me, he shuffled over to the table with his head down.

"Victor," I said, "why aren't *you* working?"

He eyed me slyly.

"Why aren't you working?"

"Fair enough. What's with the book?"

He sighed and sat across from me, dropping the book on the table. The face of our basketball hero stared back at me beneath the title: *The Gift of Jimmy V: A*

Coach's Legacy.

Jim Valvano became a legend to N.C. Sate fans after he led the Huskies to their last NCAA Championship in 1983. Victor and I had been only kids when it happened, but we both knew that tournament run by heart. We could name the scores and stats, recite the one-on-one match-ups from the first round to the Finals, up to the last-second dunk that sealed the upset. Lorenzo fucking Charles.

"Victor, why are you reading about Jim Valvano?"

"Why wouldn't I be?"

"Well, it's a book, for starters," I said. "Christ, are you that bummed we didn't make the tournament?"

"I got it bad, Johnnyboy," Victor said, pulling at his hair. "Worse than the NIT."

I frowned and fidgeted with the book's cover. Jimmy V had been famous for his coaching career, but death had turned him into a legend. There's a video of one of his speeches where he's helped up to the stage, body wracked with cancer, that Victor and I have watched 30, maybe 40 times. He limps up the steps and gives a talk that immortalizes him, and then a few months later, he dies.

I swallowed hard and looked at Victor. "Bad like Jimmy V?"

Victor nodded slowly, then looked up at me.

"Worse," he said, "at least he won a national title."

We both choked out a laugh, then the silence. Victor and I had never been good with moments like these; they were a break in our routine.

"I got it bad," he repeated, and shambled down the hall to his room. I listened to his door slowly click shut and lock, and stared into my coffee.

Carrie was quiet that evening when she heard the news.

"Christ," she whispered. "Where?"

"Right in the tit," Victor announced, prodding his chest as he walked into the room. "And fast spreading to parts unknown."

"Vic." Carrie put her hand over her mouth and leaned against the counter. "How?"

Victor shrugged and began rifling through the cupboards for coffee filters.

It was silent that night as we ate spaghetti that looked like noodles and sauce.

VII.

When my mother died two years ago, she died alone. Most of her family lived halfway across the country in Colorado, and my father had been gone since I was a kid. I had no siblings, either – that left only me by default, and I hadn't seen her in nearly a year when she died.

It's easy to say it was just too long of a drive to Asheville, that I didn't have the money or the time, but I knew even then that those were excuses.

The truth was, my mother and I never had the relationship it seemed like we should have. My dad leaving should have drawn us together, but I turned to sports instead. Growing up poor should have made me appreciate family, but instead if made me appreciate money; I worked through high school and even through college in the off-season when I should have been studying, doing all I could to meet tuition payments and avoid asking my mother for anything. I knew how much she had put on the line to take me across the state for basketball games, to make sure I had good shoes and a rim in the backyard to play on, but I never thought about moving back, not once, not even when my savings ran dangerously low.

I didn't know what to say to her, after a while. She knew where I was and I knew where she was, and that seemed like enough for me. Whatever was unsaid between us remained unsaid when she died, and I sometimes thought about what we would have talked about if I had gone back. It seemed to me I had a lot to say, though nothing specific came to mind.

Carrie didn't even let me entertain the idea of missing the funeral, driving the four hours with me and charming the socks off my aunts and cousins.

When Victor got sick, Carrie took it upon herself to make sure we were handling it like the families she saw on hospitals brochures and television sitcoms, using words like "strength" and "empathy" and "support." She referred to it as "our disease" instead of Victor's and tried making every dinner into an open forum about his health.

She assumed Victor would be open to this sort of change.

Whenever I asked Victor about his treatment, it was usually Carrie who ended up answering the question.

"It's a bibopsy," Victor explained on the eve of his first procedure.

"A biopsy," Carrie corrected from the kitchen.

I sat down on my chair in the living room with the classifieds, relieved to be only a background character in the conversation.

"What's a biopsy?"

"It's where they gut me like a fish," Victor moaned, throwing himself down on our couch.

"A biopsy is where the surgeon tests cell or tissue samples," Carrie calmly explained. She came into the living room carrying a plate of apple slices, offering them to Victor. "It's to see how far the cancer has spread and what they can do to treat it."

Victor sniffed at the tray, waving it away and pulling a fistful of sunflower seeds from his pocket instead.

"Eat an apple, Vic."

"Sveetheart, apples do not cure cancer," Victor drawled.

"Neither do sunflower seeds," Carrie said sternly. She held the tray in front of him until he took a slice.

Debating apples and sunflower seeds didn't seem quite as important once the results of the biopsy came in. I'd always thought that the stages of cancer were just part of the jargon that added drama to sitcoms, but it turns out there are real charts with survival rates and everything – and the numbers didn't look good.

Victor came home in a daze that next Friday, normally our night to play the jukebox at Duke's.

"Not tonight, darlings," he said, walking through the living room. Carrie and I eyed him from the couch; he looked pale and thin, and his Russian accent was only so-so.

"You don't want to dance, Victor?" I got up to pause *Aladdin*, Carrie's favorite movie, on the VCR, but he waved me away and turned down the hallway. We sat with the movie paused and watched him slink away toward his bedroom door, brown-paper bag clutched in his hand.

That night, Carrie and I lay silent together in our bedroom, straining our ears for sound in the dark.

VIII.

Not long after the biopsy, Victor began missing work for hospital appointments and radiation treatments. He had health insurance from the plant, but the weaker he got, the less likely seemed that he'd be able to keep his job. When he moved to part-time, Carrie and I sat down and talked about what we could do to get by. We didn't have many places to turn for help: Both of my parents were dead, and Carrie couldn't go back to her family after all that had happened.

Nobody knew whether Victor's father was dead or alive.

We sold my car to stay ahead of things; Carrie fought it all the way, but when I told her it wasn't as if I had anywhere to be in the morning, she had a hard time arguing with my logic. Providing us with an extra thousand dollars felt good, like I was finally taking care of Carrie instead of the other way around.

Lately I'd been called in for interviews with a few local businesses, and things seemed close to clicking. I followed the rules and etiquette to a T: I gave myself pep talks in the mirror beforehand, wore my best suit, delivered firm handshakes and carried my resume with me in a slick leather binder, but nothing. No callbacks, no second interviews, not even a nibble.

The worse things got, the harder Carrie tried to make them better, the more optimistic she felt she needed to be.

"It's the economy," Carrie said soothingly. "Even Victor's plant is laying workers off. There's nothing you can do but keep trying."

I would have rather she yelled.

Carrie began leaving earlier in the morning to drop Victor off at the hospital, but he preferred walking on his own. When Carrie came to his door he'd already be sitting up in bed coughing, waving her off and spitting into a tissue, tossing it into a thick heap of red on the floor near his nightstand. Instead of letting Carrie take him in, he put on layers of oil-stained flannel shirts and trekked through the cold like he did every morning before the cancer.

The physical effects of the disease – gaunt face, even thinner body, a loss of hair from the radiation – were there, but that wasn't the worst of it. The goofy accents and Victor-isms were gone; he was quieter now, often sullen, and preferred being alone.

He had already stopped answering when Carrie knocked on his door in the evening to bring him apple slices or peanut butter and celery; when she had to watch him stumble off through the snow every morning, she began to break down. She spent less time at home, picking up private tutoring jobs after school to help with Victor's portion of the rent. I stayed home, keeping him company and cooking his meals – for the first time, it seemed a good thing that I didn't have anywhere to be.

I pulled my chair into his room and the two of us watched college ball together again, grateful that at least winter meant we weren't missing out on much at the local courts.

"John, do you really want to know about my dad?" Victor asked me one day, muting the television.

The question took me by surprise.

"I don't know. If you want to tell me."

"I don't want to tell you."

"That's fine."

"I don't want to talk about it."

"That's fine, Vic."

"I don't."

"Then let's watch the game."

Victor turned to look at me, his hand gripping the television remote. His movements seemed slow and clunky, like his limbs might get tangled up together. He had grown thin, even thinner than before, and his beautiful floppy hair was now nothing more than a bald cap. I saw wetness around his eyes.

I knew Victor would tell me everything I'd wanted to know. It was clear there was something here after all, that it wasn't all just jokes and dancing – under all that hair and through those accents there was pain and memory and something to say. I could picture it all pouring out, tears down his cheek and his hand gripping mine. The silence made me nervous.

I swallowed hard and turned back to the television. I felt weak, and I could feel

Victor's eyes burning into my temple. He unmuted the television, and we watched the rest of the game in silence.

Later, I cooked him a grilled cheese sandwich and delivered it to his bedside.

"John," he said, rubbing his head, "this looks like a grilled cheese sandwich."

"That's what it is, Victor."

He stared into the melting cheese.

When Carrie came home that night, she sat at his bedside and watched him sleep. After a few minutes, Victor opened his eyes. From the hallway, I watched her put her hand on his chest.

"Do you hurt, Victor?"

"Yes."

IX.

Carrie was the one to find him.

She went into his room to bring him a glass of juice one morning before work, and when she came to wake me afterward – pulling me out of bed and then collapsing into my arms – her hands were dyed a sticky orange.

I rubbed her back, slurred apologies into her hair while my eyes adjusted to the light. Her head was buried in my chest, shaking as she tried to make words through the sobs.

I walked over to Victor's bedside while Carrie washed up. He was lying on his side, one hand hanging off the side of the bed. Standing over him like that, seeing him colorless and stiff and pinned to the bed by his checkered blue bed sheets, I wanted to cry. I wanted to cry for my family and cry for my cousin and cry for the cancer that left him all cut up inside. I wanted to cry for his drunk father, and for my dead father, too, and even for Carrie's poor white-haired mother, running her hands over rosary beads in a big, empty church with gaudy stained-glass windows. I wanted to cry because I knew she wouldn't pray for us.

I pinched the bridge of my nose and closed my eyes. I pulled the bed sheet over Victor's head, walked away and closed the door behind me. I cried ghost tears and wiped them with arms I didn't have.

Carrie stepped out of the bathroom looking foggy-eyed and damp. Together we walked into the living room, sat down and talked. She was out of sick days from taking Victor to his first hospital visits, so for her there was nothing to do but go to work. I promised her I would take care of everything. That I would call the coroner for Victor, that I would start making plans to raise money for a funeral. I promised her we'd be okay – I would have promised her the moon if I thought it would help.

She packed her things for school, and we hugged at the door. I kissed her on the cheek and tasted salt, told her I loved her. As she walked out the door and into the apartment stairwell, I thought to myself that I had never seen a person look so much like a wilted flower.

After she left, I sat at the table with a cup of coffee and listened the rest of the world wake. The street was already thrumming with traffic, and our neighbors were scraping off their windshields in the carports. A dog was barking beneath me on the first floor. In our apartment, the only sound was the ticking of the glass coffeepot heating on the counter. It seemed impossible that Victor was gone, that in the second bedroom down the hallway on the left, my cousin went to sleep last night and didn't wake up.

I thumbed through the phone book looking for the right number to call. The whole thing felt like part of a sick standup routine. *What do you do with the body of your dead cousin?* I kept thinking of the poor old ladies at Duke's who must be wondering by now where their floppy-haired friend has been. I tried to cry and vomited coffee and bile into the sink instead.

At half past ten I made the call, and 30 minutes later three men came and took Victor away. I stood at the top of the steps and watched them go; the tightly zipped black bag that was my cousin stayed stiff as a bedpost as they maneuvered it down the apartment stairwell.

X.

The two of us were completely disjointed without Victor around. Carrie stayed up too late crying, waking bleary-eyed and unorganized, scrambling in the morning for her papers and bags. I spent too much time drinking coffee and trying to think of anything but death. No matter what, I always ended up on Victor – with all the talking he did, I thought mostly about what he didn't say. The heavy silences between us toward the end, the things he had wanted to share only when he thought he was supposed to. It was really his presence I missed the most, the remnants of his faux Russian accent still knocking around the walls. The echo of his broomstick on the floor.

Carrie stopped cooking, and for weeks we picked at cereal and vegetables, living off the crumbs of our former lives. We bought cheap fast food until the bags piled up in our trashcan, and the kitchen table disappeared under newspapers, magazines and Carrie's binders and workbooks for class.

I had dreams that I was drowning in a grease fryer, my skin bubbling and tearing, sliding off the bone as I swam for shore. When I got there, my hands burned and slipped off the edge of the fryer, repelling me back toward the center, where I floundered and burned. Sometimes Victor appeared next me, gaunt and calm as he melted.

Weeks later, I woke from one of these dreams to hear Carrie crying in the bathroom. Normally she was gone before I woke, but hearing her sobs shocked me into

Illustration by Stephen Smith

consciousness. It sounded at first like she had collapsed, but I then recognized the pounding that was her fists on the sink, the retching of her face over cold porcelain. My heart skipped beats in the moments she was silent, a whispered scream, the dry heaves and empty gasps for air. And then it was done. The sound of toilet paper whirring on the roll, a door clicking shut and she was gone before I had lifted the covers from my chest.

That evening, I cooked dinner for the first time since Carrie had moved in. We didn't have much; I rifled through the cupboards, tossing boxes of stale cereal and loose bits of pasta in the trash, trying to piece together a meal. I found frozen hamburger and defrosted it with hot water in the sink. There was an unopened box of hard taco shells and a half bag of seasoning in the cupboard behind the pasta, and a plastic baggie of shredded cheese in the refrigerator. I wasn't much of a cook, but the instructions on the back of the taco box were numbered and easy to read. I stirred the seasoning in slowly and took extra care not to burn the meat.

Carrie came home around 5 o'clock and smiled when she saw the taco platter. She sat down with me, and the two of us ate a meal together for the first time since Victor died. We talked about her students, the leads I had for jobs, dancing around his name. When we did talk about him, we laughed, remembering the way he blinked when he was confused, the odd aphorisms he offered in the face of questions he didn't know how to answer. His answers seemed so much wiser to us now.

Carrie kissed me on the cheek afterward, and I began to make dinner every night.

My meals were cheap and simple, starchy enough to get us through to the next day. I bought hamburger helper meals or made chicken and noodles. Beef and rice. Bread and meat. Carrie's moods never seemed to improve much from one day to the next, but she began to look healthier, less bleary and wilted and more like a living thing.

A little more than a month later, I was called in for a second interview for a management position at a paper company in Durham. The boss was a nice old man with a deceptively strong handshake and a repertoire of bad jokes that can only come from many years of being a grandfather. He showed me pictures of all five of them and talked about his youngest son, a laid-off carpenter whose wife was expecting their second child in a few weeks. He smiled when he said it, told me he hoped to retire soon and buy a home near them, just to keep an eye on things.

He talked to me more like a grandfather than a boss – not in a condescending way, but in a kind one. We needed money now more than ever, but I didn't feel desperate in this man's office, a modest gray room with a desk filled more with picture frames than paper. I shook his hand when I left, and he told me he'd be in touch. I said I sure hoped he would.

By the time I made it home that evening Carrie was already sleeping, but I woke the next morning to the smell of breakfast. I walked into the kitchen and wrapped my arms around her waist from behind. I kissed her on the neck and she smiled.

She was staring blankly at the lumpy disks of batter in the pan. There were bubbles forming on the surface, and the discs were morphing into small, mountainous globs.

"Carrie," I said, "those look like muffins."

"Well, they're pancakes," she replied, sprinkling blueberries in the batter.

One Block Off Bourbon
Matt Dennison

The finger-snapping man
guiding people into
the nightclub with
slicked-back hair and
winning ways sits
on the toilet
head down drunk
       old
tuxedo on a nail
as the street follows
him up the stairs
up the stairs
into his
room and down
the stairs down
the stairs into
the street
while
down the hall
in a room
five feet wide
and twelve feet long
with one wall green
and one wall purple,
yellow door and
window black,
I lie in bed
admiring
the baby roaches
that climb my walls
and wonder about myself
for liking them
as the lights
and the noise
and the knowing
all fade.

A Difference
Matt Dennison

Working in the 5 a.m. New Orleans shipyard,
scraping the inner-hulls of monstrous
river-gone grain haulers after
the other midnight-
ending job—

orange rust showering below and beyond
and upon us

we pause to watch from fifty-foot ladders
the Korean crew execute
their militaristic assault upon
their own spotless
deck.

So tiny! So fast!

And strangely
vicious.

Yes, then.

We return to our union-slow chiseling of rust,
sweeping of water and
hot private dreams

of being

fired and finally
sleeping the sleep
of the damned
and the
free.

Like a Bull
Katie Burgess

In biology class you focus on the video, not that you need to, not while your teacher practices his putting stroke out in the hallway. Parents here frown on biology for the most part—all that Darwin and reproduction and whatnot—so your school doesn't stress it too much. Instead you watch tapes about drug abuse or personal hygiene or self-esteem while Mr. Davis hits balls into a plastic cup.

Craig Kimbell, who sits beside you, reaches across your desk to swat Missy Grant on the arm. "Hey," Craig says. "Hey. I talked to Nate this morning. He said he enjoyed last night."

Missy keeps her eyes on the video, as if anxious to know what happens next to the angel dust kid.

"He said you rode him like a bull."

Heads turn. Missy's jaw clenches. It takes you a second to understand. At first you hear it as, "He says you rode him likeable," which makes no sense. Then it hits you. The class quiets, anticipating its first ever actual biology lesson.

Craig grins. "Yeah. He said you rode him like a goddamn bull."

Missy whips around and glares. Her face reddens, but not, you think, from embarrassment. You slouch, trying to get out of their way, but neither of them even notices you. "My sex life," Missy says, "is none of your business." Craig laughs but can't seem to think of a comeback. People go back to their conversations and games of hangman. The moment ends, for everyone but you.

You attend the same Baptist church as most of the town. They teach that lusting in your heart counts as sin, which is why you constantly replace all your dirty thoughts with images of trees or the ocean. You know that Missy has gone astray; still, you can't help admiring her a little. My sex life is none of your business. No denials, no shame. My sex life. Missy, while only fifteen, like you, has had sex. Has a sex life. One that involves riding someone like a bull.

Years later, in college, you find yourself entwined with your boyfriend in his narrow dorm bed, which smells of nachos. After months of wheedling, he's managed to get your top off.

"Baby, tell me your fantasies," whispers the naked, freckled boy, a sophomore in public relations. Your actual fantasies, though, thanks to years of repression, tend towards the abstract. A single wave caressing the beach, the wind blowing against your skirt. Then you remember a certain phrase, one you sometimes repeat to yourself at night, the closest thing to a bona fide fantasy you can muster. You say, "I want to ride you like a bull."

You expect it to please him, but he pulls away. He stares at you, as if some succubus has replaced the Baptist virgin he'd hoped to seduce. He goes limp.

"Or, you know, whatever," you say, pulling up the covers.

He kisses your forehead. "Look, you don't need to impress me," he says. "I love your innocence." In two weeks, he will leave you for a Catholic.

Later, as he falls asleep, you think about Missy Grant and wonder what she's up to these days. You imagine her in a red dress, blowing kisses. You wait for your boyfriend's snores. You reach between your legs, saying to yourself, *like a bull. Like a bull.*

Melancholy
Michael Diebert

A landscape of some expanse, perfectly flat,
stretched out, flowerless, no rain or sun,
hard beige dirt going on and on
until it smacks into slate sky,
windless, treeless, no extremes,
cold and heat in perfect deadlock,
rocky, a little treacherous at first
but familiar in time, the fissures,
and always, always some slight measure
of light. Uncanny, how easy for me
to get here, how easy for me to stay
a long time and never want to leave,
how easy to block the memory of mountains
and the rush that mountains afford,
to hoard love as though it were grain
and me an impregnable silo,
how easy to believe myself relieved
of the river, no water here
and no container to pour it in,
no wildlife, no humankind, just me
rolling around in the folds of my own head.
I am alive because I am not dead.

Lightning Bugs
Michael Diebert

Hot slap-happy grass-stained knee-skinned no-wind kind of night.
Greg and Robert James and Denise leaping,
lunging with grunts and mason jars in the dark
in Mr. and Mrs. Childress's wild backyard.
Jenny and me, weeds half up to our knees, chasing the dog
into and back out of the porch light,
mosquitoes trumpeting in my ear—
Greg's got one. Denise another.
They run to the fence's edge and compare. Little conspirators.
See, me and Jenny
we don't need a jar or a hand,
just our eyes. They're just like little stars,
little flashlights lighting the way
for all the other bugs. They flare, disappear,
just like when Jenny smiles then doesn't
at a dumb joke. Her teeth are bright white
and the way she sometimes sparkles in my direction,
I know for a fact
the block is way too dull to hold her back.

Letter to Ferris from Decatur
Michael Diebert

Good Jim: A rare fog this a.m. The backlit trees guard their secrets.
Single leaves dangle from branches like Christmas ornaments.
Our friend Hopkins had it right—the world is charged. I don't want
to write another word about not being able to write. Toledo
treats you well, I trust. Is life still full? I'm still doing the work
I was meant to do, still brushing the scales from my students' eyes.
Egg is to yolk as work is to disappointment. When I take care
to remember that, I enjoy myself. Of course I enjoy myself
more when I can sit here, watch the vapor from my coffee,
look out the window, and read meaning into the rain-sheen
on the deck. Me and my little poems. Pain is hard to do
justice to. One of many reasons I am in awe of you. Re politics,
I live on a blue island in a sea of red. Progressive. Cozy.
Give me a beer on the patio at one of our lovely pubs: that's policy
I can get behind. Let's see. Our last meeting was in Chinatown,
the Evergreen, that dyed-in-the-wool old-school joint
beneath the concrete moan of the Stevenson. It was cold.
I remember zip about the food. We were tired, enervated
from two days of full immersion in the river of words,
words, and more words. Scrape of silverware, passing of platters.
You recommended a book which I later read and quite enjoyed.
We were talking about fame. That conference can be an ego-
stroke or -blow. Or both. "Thank God for anonymity," you said.
I nodded heartily and resumed looking at my plate.
I've met myself a lot in my life. Do we live in Venn diagrams?
There I go. I need to be Bukowski-loud, Ginsberg-garrulous.
But the world is also charged with silent, eloquent gestures:
our server's tiny, embarrassed smile, the iridescent fish
going nowhere, cutting clean angles in the humming, bubbling water.
The fish tank of language. Jim, I wish to swim with that much purpose.
We ate until we were sated. We paid the bill. We walked back
across Wentworth to your car, got in, drove to the reading,
and sat respectfully in the back. This is the world. Anonymity:
I hear you, but I have to think on it. Keep life full. All best, Michael.

Like a Burst of Fire
Jackson Culpepper

Henry was not on the baseball team and he had only ever been to one game. Really he was not a man for sport at all, but when Fred came by in his new flatbed and blew the horn, something in Henry jumped up before he even knew what it was.

"What's all this racket for?" Henry asked Fred.

Fred whispered as though his trip was a conspiracy, "Southeastern division! Delia beat the whole goddamn South. They're having a victory party at the river. Word is our Reds have that place taken over." Fred grinned. "Look in the back, Henry."

Henry lifted a flap of canvas to reveal several cases of beer. He quickly pulled the flap back, hoping the neighbors didn't see. His was a good Methodist neighborhood.

Ula Mae, Fred's sister, leaned over from the passenger side and said, "I heard they have champagne and a full band. You will dance, won't you, Henry?"

"What, in the water?" Fred asked, cocking his hat back on his head. "It's a pool, not some joint."

"They're wild, they might. Remember when they started that big fight in Americus halfway through the eighth inning? The radio said it was utter chaos. You were listening, weren't you, Henry?" Ula Mae said.

Henry had been listening to the Carter Family on the Opry all evening.

"Come on Henry, let's go. You don't get out enough."

Henry got his clothes. On his way back way out, his mother asked, "Who is making such a racket in the drive?"

"Just an acquaintance. I shall not be long."

"Do not stay out too late, the bishop will be at service tomorrow."

"Yes ma'am."

Fred slapped the steering wheel when Henry squeezed in between him and Ula Mae. Soon the wide streets and well-kept lawns faded to woods and shotgun houses west of town.

"Feel around, under the seat, Henry, see if you find anything," Fred said.

Henry bent and reached under the seat. There was a half-full half-pint jar. "That's the good stuff," Fred said, "some of Pappy Marlowe's. Go on, try a sip." Henry flushed. He imagined his Mother's and the bishop's scowls, foregrounded against the church's white doorway.

"Well let me try it, if you won't," said Ula Mae, taking the jar. She took a dainty sip and then a longer one. Fred chuckled. "Old Marlowe's whiskey will come up on you about like he would—sweet and smooth, but before you know it, you're face to face with an old swamp runner. And he don't let go easy."

"Oh Fred, hush," Ula Mae said, turning to Henry. "He always gets like that, every time I drink any little thing! He starts all this seduction talk."

"Just trying to protect your innocence, Uly," Fred said.

Ula Mae took another sip. "I don't know what innocence you think you have, what with that letter you sent to Gladys and all this whiskey in Daddy's new truck—which you borrowed without asking—and I don't even need to mention that woman on Coney road—"

"Woman, be silent!"

They hit a pothole and lurched, coming down in a flurry of elbows, shoulders and half of old Marlowe's liquor. Fred started to explain, "It was just a sappy old love letter Gladys held on to for no damn reason."

"She always was sentimental," Henry said.

"And Pa said I could take it out; I'll have to haul cotton in it anyway."

"It does take some practice to learn the gears," Henry said.

"Oh Henry, don't take up for him like that," Ula Mae said.

"Do you want to swim across the river?" Fred asked.

"You wouldn't kick me out of a borrowed truck."

Fred and Ula Mae kept going until they came to the landing. Bubba Evans came out of his shack. "One dollar, mister," he said, and Fred handed him a silver dollar. Bubba dragged the cable to pull them across the river.

Over the slosh of water, Henry heard dance music, shouting. Electric lights reflected in the ripples of the river. The pool was a beacon, bounded by shadowed water. "There is music, I told you there would be!" said Ula Mae.

The ferry slid up the bank and Fred drove off and parked by a bus. "The Reds' own bus, Henry!" he said, slapping the side of it.

They walked through the gate of the pool into a gold-lit world of noise. The water seethed with hairy-chested men and suited women. Arms lifted brown bottles of beer. A handful of musicians played ragtime—Henry recognized Bissett on trombone and Leon on trumpet. Beyond them, he did not recognize half the people there. For all he knew, and it seemed so, half of Georgia was in that pool.

"Suit up, Henry," called Fred.

"I could not find mine," Henry said. In truth, he did not own one.

"Just jump in in your underwear." Many of the men and even a few of the women had done so. Henry felt out of place in his shirtsleeves and hat. A man in shorts bumped into him. "Have some hooch," the man said through a red forest of beard. Henry took the pint jar and sipped, thinking liquor might help him loosen up. Finding himself among such a rowdy crowd and already so much sin, he might as well drink. Fire with fire, sin with sin. The liquor burned but he made himself drink two good swigs before he handed it back to the man and thanked him.

Henry stripped to his shorts. He folded his clothes and placed them on a bench in a far corner, his hat set atop them. The pool was packed; man against woman, skin against skin. There was an unopened beer on the bench. Henry took it and slid into the pool.

Pushing through the wet mass of bodies, Henry searched for Fred and Ula Mae, or anybody he might know. Finding no one, he turned to a group of four men, one of them in a Reds baseball cap, and introduced himself. He told them he was from Delia and asked where they were from. They were all quite drunk, but Henry could not leave just after he had made introductions. One man said "From Valdosta, all the way up here to celebrate."

"That ain't nothing, I came from Athens."

"The hell with Athens, I came from Ocala."

"What the hell you here from Ocala for?"

"To watch baseball, dumbass, why else?"

Henry was not sure if they were joking or about to fight.

Henry grabbed a passing liquor jar and took a deep few swigs. He left the baseball group and looked for women to talk to. Three of them stood sipping beer and he pushed through warm bodies to get to them.

Breaking into their circle, Henry saw that Ula Mae. "Isn't it wild?" she said.

"Yes, it is," he said, but he was not sure if she heard him since they were adjacent to the band and Bissett had played a loud gliss. Ula Mae made swift introductions, of which Henry remembered none. Then Ula Mae filled any possible silence with gossip about Fred and Gladys: how she jilted him or he jilted her. Henry was not sure which. He turned to one of the other girls and said, "Did you travel far to be here tonight?"

"What?"

"Where are you from?"

"My girlfriend and I came down from Vienna."

"I am from—" Henry began, but a trombone slide stuck into the space between them. The girl's eyes crossed looking at it, before it disappeared back the way it came.

"I need to find my friend," the girl said. "She always does something wild at parties like this. I have to keep an eye on her. It was good to meet you." And she pushed through bodies and was gone. Ula Mae still talked.

Henry tried vaguely to follow the girl. Hands clapped him on the back. He saw things terribly clearly, when he looked directly at them. Everybody was golden in the electric lights. Others laughed and it made Henry laugh. His ideas against drink and debauchery were changing rapidly. Still, he wanted to talk to a woman. Talk, and bring her over and sit by the fire, listening to the Opry. More than anything, he wanted some girl to call on, to take out. Henry had the handicap of shyness and the constraint of a zealous mother, not that those things should really be stopping him.

Then and there, he vowed to relax his strenuous life and live like he imagined one of these revelers lived. At least in part. He took another drink.

By now he was used to the noise, sweat, men yelling and girls giggling, and him pushing his way among them, looking for that first girl he had talked to, or another one whom he could talk to. He heard a laugh like back-porch chimes, and turned. There was a woman laughing, her hair curled and untouched by the water, her skin the color of honey in the lights. Her eyes were dark, were as comfortable in this place, probably in any place, as Henry was apprehensive. She was happy here only because it was here. He pushed towards her, focusing his failing concentration on her, until Fred grabbed him by the arm.

Fred leaned against the pool edge, smoking a cigar. "Did you hear what she said?" Fred asked.

"She only laughed, I was trying to—"

"Ula Mae's told everyone from here to Carolina about Gladys, inventing half of it and blowing the other half up big as the moon. She's even spilling out every terrible rumor that's gone around about . . . Coney Road . . . you didn't hear her?"

"She was," Henry belched, "talking."

Fred colored violently and struck the water and called Ula Mae a name that Henry would never repeat.

"She can walk back to town then—swim! I'll pay Bubba not to let her back on the ferry. She can't just go and tell all about that—Hell, she's Gladys' friend too, they go to goddamn Sunday school together," Fred said. He grabbed his hat, shoving it into Henry's chest as he spoke. "This is the way they are, these women, Henry: nothing but mouths with pretty legs. She's jealous of Gladys, I'll tell you, she can't stand a girl with pretty blond hair like that. She'd tear it all out if she could and laugh about it afterward. What do you think, can't you see it? Can't you tell it about her?"

Henry took a jar from beside Fred and drank a long swallow of whiskey. Fred stopped him, his eyed wide and focused toward the diving board. Henry turned. The woman he saw before stood there, nude, bathed in the dull light. All the water stilled and all the rowdy cries ceased. She stood like a goddess carved in honey-colored stone, as though polished marble held all the delicate curves along her hips, or else she was a tongue of flame solidified, swelling and tapering. Her face was unashamed, bearing a small smile not of drunk wildness but of quiet uncruel mischief. In that gleaming sliver of time, she looked at Henry in a way that bathed light into every part of him; not desire, nor lust, but a warmth that would remain forever, smoldering, wakened to flame every now and then or dying down, but never extinguished. Henry watched every sinew in her frame shift as she dove, disappearing without a splash into the water, her feet kicking up like a last burst of fire. He barely heard the hoots and jeers as she swam the length of the pool and rose on the other side, where the woman from Vienna covered her with a towel. She blew a kiss and faded beyond the water and people and debauchery and extinguished from sight.

Illustration by Stephen Smith

Fred didn't speak. Henry pushed through the bodies. Shoved through them, he realized, but it was not from anger so he did not say "Pardon me" as he had the whole night.

He passed Ula Mae, who said "Henry have you seen Fred?"

Henry said, "Yes, and you should avoid it."

Bissett's slide blocked him for a moment and he pushed it back, making an off-key slur that Bissett worked into the song anyhow.

Henry passed the baseball men from Valdosta and Athens and Ocala. They yelled gibberish. Henry gently pushed one aside like a door and pushed him back after he had passed through.

Finally, Henry climbed out of the pool. The red-bearded man was still sitting on the bench with a jar of whiskey. Henry said, "Where did that girl go?"

"Girl?"

"The one from the diving board."

"How'd she dive with so many people?"

"Sheer beauty. You didn't see her? She swam through and came out right here."

"Have some hooch."

Around the edge of the pool there were only couples, or drunks sleeping, or the shining brass of the band.

Outside the sounds were muted. A large moon hung and flickered in the sloshing of the river. No one was out there. Henry would have called out, but he never learned either of their names.

On the ride home, Fred said through clenched teeth, "Uly, I told you not to talk any more about me and Gladys. It ain't nothing to talk about."

"Who told you that? I didn't say a single word, except the bald facts of it."

"Bullshit. You were blabbing about it to everybody! What's going to happen when she hears about it?"

"For one thing, she'll be glad she didn't end up with a bastard like you."

"Woman! Take that back, or God so help me—"

"Fred, shut your damned mouth," said Henry. Ula Mae and Fred stared at him, jaws slack. Henry continued, "I'm sick of hearing you two. All this hatefulness turns my stomach."

Fred mumbled. Ula Mae sighed. They didn't speak any more on the way to take Henry home.

The next day, Henry woke up late and told his mother he would not be attending services that day.

"But Henry, the bishop will be there."

"A bishop isn't that special. I'll go next time he stops by."

He drove out to the river and went to get his hat from where he'd forgotten it on the bench. Henry tried to picture the woman on the diving board again, and he felt, lighter within him, that same warmth he felt when she looked at him. But by then she wasn't a thing for picturing. He crossed the ferry and headed towards Vienna.

Three Stanzas for Luis J. Rodriguez
Mario Duarte

I. ¡Qué Viva La Raza!
On the window sill, the goldfish plant blossoms swim in orange relief. Their minty green leaves calm that evil serpent, the mind, and flow beyond the waves of sunlight. They hear the immigrant's son say, "Is this not my country?" "No," their small voices answer. "There will never be a place for you on this earth."

II. ¡Aqui Estoy!
Fingers and toes, arms and legs, fight loneliness, but realize this dear old sausages love floats out of our lips on the white sail of rapidly expelled words. They carry the heaviest cargo loads in their hulls but nothing calms the earthquake generated tsunami they must face, for nothing of what we are can ever survive love.

III. Change is a mother!
I was always a skinny, little dude—eating my dreams. I explored continents of the imagination, shouldering a stick-gun, treading the tall weeds along the Hennepin canal, other days I was an astronaut dangling like a spider hanging by a web in the deep black of space. Even today, if you touch my shoulder blades I will flinch into light.

101 Degrees
Mario Duarte

Here in Durham, North Carolina the sweat cascade from my forehead stinging my eyes, and the scratch you left on my cheek stings—the hour bobs in the yellow sea inside me.

Heat waves ripple the leaves dangling from the trees, like snakes dropping, until the faceless sky rips apart and the red rain explodes splashing even the dust into bloody droplets.

I hold my hands up to the red rain. Let its density migrate down my palms. Skeleton-white lightning zigzags from blue-black clouds, until they churn with your blue eyes.

Locked Trunk to Trunk
Mario Duarte

Once we were elephants locking trunks. We thought it would always be this way. Even today I bought you a Birthday card—two squirrels face each other, holding a nut between them.

Last night, a spider hung from a web. It dangled against the backdrop of night like an astronaut space walking—only a thin white line shot from her abdomen suspended her fate.

Later, when I returned, her web was complete: a net to catch everything from the tiniest, virtually invisible insects to your face trapped in the sticky lines, your fingers ripping the web apart.

Grounded
Tyler Dennis

Ask me to remember that night, and I'd tell you that it was the shock at seeing my mother half-naked that rattled me most. She was always so pruned back then. Made up like a politician's wife, hair permed to a dizzying height, lips masked by a shade of deep red, and breasts fully supported by the priciest bra in three counties.

Her hair was flattened on one side and frayed on the other by what little sleep she'd had before. Half her face was red and her eyes were black with unruly eye makeup. She was bra-less and wore an oversized tee-shirt that said "Yellow Dog Democrat" on the front with a yellow dog fighting a bite-sized Republican elephant underneath. Her breasts rested just below the text on her shirt and seemed to have a volatile structure to them like the yellow part of an uncooked egg.

Between sips of coffee, she puffed on her Camel non-filter. There was a drone coming from the television that was interrupted by canned laughter from a studio audience. I couldn't tell you what was on. The TV was an eerie spotlight that seemed to illuminate everything but my mother's face. There was something distinctly unlady-like about her cross-legged positioning.

Her voice was soft when she spoke.

"Are you?"

I tried to play it all off as a joke; I spoke to her like she was taking this all too seriously. "Everything will be all right. It isn't so terrible." I cooed.

"You can't do this to me tonight. You're mine. You're my baby, and I just want to hold you. If you pull away from me again, I'll knock you down," she said matter-of-factly.

I didn't move. Not due to the threat of violence, but just because she deserved to hold onto something that would be gone after that night. If I took her at her word, then I was her science, her scripture in one fleshly, 5'11 form. That night, she lost both.

For the rest of the night, her vocal cords were a venue for every cliché on the cliché dais. She asked me if anyone ever bullied with me at school? Answer: yes. Had any of her half-forgotten ex-boyfriends ever touched me when I was small? Answer: no. Was it because she had divorced my father? Answer: no. How long had I known?

"Since I was three years old." I said, my chin positioned awkwardly on her shoulder. The words fell directly into her ear.

By then, she was sleepy-eyed. My responses were limited to one or two words; our voices were low when we dared to puncture the murmur of studio audience. Most frequently, I would assure her that everything would be okay.

"No it won't." she said and then added something like "You'll never have babies" or "I feel like I'm burying you."

"I promise it will." I lied. But I didn't feel so guilty because she was already gone.

"You don't care what you put people through. I should have you locked up in a crazy house."

The late night talk show host continued to steal cautious glances at his starlet-guest's breasts.

◆

A few hours later, and the sun rose red. My mother was in the kitchen, fishing through drawers with near-comic ferocity.

Once she'd found the sliver of notebook paper with a phone number written on it, our kitchen looked crippled by the effort. Someone had played a game of Rook on the kitchen table with a natural disaster.

We were never close with my mother's mother ("Mom's mom" when we were feeling affectionate). I never knew exactly which day in March was her birthday. For most of my childhood, she was unnoticeably not there. For most of my *mother's* childhood, too, she was a missing face on a milk carton. Every Mother's Day, Mom would make this huge deal about Papaw, getting him cards and taking us to see him.

"He was my mommy *and* my *dead-y*." She would say, fully aware of how schmaltzy she sounded. Sometimes, tears would follow. My mother has always been a crier.

My mother didn't care for her because she wasn't warm in the way that many old women are; she was the type of person who would watch *Terms of Endearment* and say "Darn, that's sad" rather than producing actual tears. If you didn't cry, my mother didn't trust you.

The morning after Mom found out about me, she pored over the scattered papers in our kitchen for this mystery woman's number before calling it.

The two talked for only a little while, in sentences that were hacked into "*Ummhmm's*" and "*I understand's*." Whenever my mother said goodbye, it was like she'd been talking to a bill collector she was cordial with.

"Hey, *hey*! Are we ready, sportsfan?" My mom's mom said, throwing a cigarette outside her car window. "When you get in, babe, be sure to roll that window back up." Can't waste good air conditioning, I inferred.

I'd always loved the gap between her front teeth because it made her different. Her hair was cut swimming cap short, and she had a goggle-shaped tan line around her eyes. The summer before, she had bought this new above-ground pool, my egocentric mother theorized, in a big to get closer to us; since then, her skin had been the color of bread crust.

We both knew that she wasn't taking me out for lunch. She was there to tell me things that my mother couldn't. Maybe a few things that Mom didn't even know to say.

"I'm gonna tell it to you straight. It doesn't make one bit of difference to me what you are—whether or not you like men, women, or crepe suzette. But just know that if you are like that you can't be that way here. It was stupid of you to tell people, let them find out, whatever."

It took me a few seconds to recover from how blunt that was. Whenever I saw her, usually the script was always the same—"Do you miss school?", "What are you going to do for work?" or "Have you read any good books lately?". She wasn't being cruel and there was no edge to her words. She was stating facts that I knew already.

"I wasn't planning on staying here." I tried my best to sound detached. My arms were crossed, and I slouched in my seat, hoping all this added to my air of angsty indifference.

She nodded, eyes on the road. "Well, that's good. Where do you see yourself then?"

This woman had never changed any of my diapers. She had eyes that were unblemished by sentimental images of me with baby booties or with an umbilical cord anchor. She spoke to me more like a man than anyone else ever had. I gave her leeway because of it.

"I don't know. Not here."

"You have to be more specific. Atlanta? Chattanooga? Somewhere bigger—New York?"

"Maybe New York," I shrugged.

"Hmm. What will you *do* in New York? You'll pay six times as much to live in New York than it costs to live here."

"Write comics, maybe. I'm not good as an artist, but I'm okay." I'd never told anyone that before and I shouldn't have started with her. Old people have this way of prying into your plans for the future, pointing out just how unrealistic they are, and seeming all too pleased with themselves when they get you to reconsider any sort of extraordinary future for yourself. With every dream that your heart and mind births, their response is always similar: "What are you going to do if that doesn't work out? Okay, well that then? You'll be eating cat food if you don't have anything else in mind."

Old people are too grounded in reality. And being grounded is the next closest thing to being buried.

"Why did you come today?" I ask with all the good manners of a teacher's pet. A spiteful part of me wanted to see this woman squirm.

She smiled at me. "Your mama thinks that this will pass. That if she doesn't talk about it or think about it, it won't happen. She didn't say as much, but I know her well enough.

"Don't throw it up into her face just yet, okay? This is all alphabet soup to her—nothing is clear or spelled out in way that she can understand. She's still young enough to think that people are only different because they chose to be, to aggravate or to annoy her. I understand, though. I'm old enough that I know people, and I know that they don't ever really change."

"So I should just trust you for no reason?"

"No. Why in God's name would you do that? I've given you no reason to trust me, sports fan." She reached over to slap my knee in a show of camaraderie; words can't describe how uncomfortable this made me feel.

"Should we eat now or later?" she asked. "I'd like to take you somewhere."

By eleven that morning, we were at a place called Deer Head Cemetery. It was quiet there, as places inhabited by dead sons-a-bitches tend to be. We stopped at a grave that was more concrete paperweight than tombstone. The man in the ground had worked with her at a mill a few years back, she said, before correcting herself.

"Maybe ten."

There was regret in those words that implied that those ten years had come and gone like birthday money.

"During weekends he dressed and wore makeup like a woman, went to a club in Birmingham and danced to songs by Donna Summer. He was the only man who didn't work on machines at the mill.

"Everyone knew what he was. Some of the girl's didn't want him folding with us, weren't comfortable around him. He had eyebrows thin like toothpicks and that scared us because we didn't understand why. The first words I said to him was asking him why, and he said, I'll never forget, 'Because I only draw them on when there's someone worth looking good for.' He thought I was making fun."

I knew where this was headed. My back was hot with anger, as if both she and this dead man were ganging up on me, preaching to me. It was the fear of being outnumbered. I could feel sweat rising up on my arms even under the shade of a sycamore.

"I don't know what makes you think you have the right but you don't." I wasn't comfortable enough in her company to get truly acidic. But there was still bite in my words as I turned away and walked back to the car. Finding that the door was locked, I settled for sitting on the dirt underneath my shoes. From there, you could see most of the cemetery.

The wrought-iron gate was detailed for a Podunk graveyard—*Deer Head Cemetery* in what looked like Thomas Jefferson's best penmanship. Just above that was an arrow pointing up to the heavens with curlicues at the arrow's base.

She had carried a blanket out to the gravesite. When I thought to look to her, she was sitting on it, still next to that grave. That man, whoever he was, died from the disease that is prone to killing men who sleep with other men.

I didn't want to hear about him. What would've been the point when I already knew how things ended for him? I didn't feel like bonding with her over a dead man who had little in common with me to begin with.

Part of me hated that man for bringing something I'd thought didn't happen in Rainsville to the forefront of my thoughts. I didn't know that it reached so far as Northeast Alabama.

I sighed. I had no right to be mad at her. Or a dead man, least of all. My body, full of knots before, seemed to unwind with this realization and a slight squall of breeze seemed to fan me back to her. My standing shadow engulfed her.

"You should move over some so that you're not in the sun so much." I suggested.

"As if a knockout like me is worried about sun exposure." Then she smiled as if to deliberately show off every line on her face. The gap between her front teeth looked welcoming, like a door left opened.

"Tell me about him. Will you?" I asked, because it then struck me that we weren't there for me. If she told me about him, about how he had died alone, then maybe that was her way of protecting me, exonerating herself, and honoring his memory all at once.

"There were other men, he said, that danced at the bars that he went to. But they did it as a joke and looked like something out of a circus show, had voices like gravel and told dirty jokes to shock people into laughing. Difference was, he really wanted to be a woman. When she—he always told us to call him that—died, no one here knew what to do with him. Her family was a good God-fearing, church-going bunch. Her brother was a Baptist preacher, of course, and the sister-in-law was a teacher at your school.

"They didn't pay for a burial. I never knew where she was buried, wasn't even in the papers. But one day, I came here on a whim, looking for the kind of conversation that living folks are incapable of. Since then, this has been her grave. For me, anyway."

"There's moss growing out of the fracture thingies in the marker. It's so old." I ran my hands along the velvety texture of the moss and then the unforgiving stone. "It can't really be his, can it?"

"You're right, it isn't. But it's nice to have a place to bring fake flowers."

I nodded in agreement, swatting at a grasshopper that had landed on my leg, then looked down to see a plagues-worth of them insect-ing around with their diving rod antennaes and grass-green bodies.

"Course he did make-up better'n anybody at that damn mill. During lunch break he would make-over some of the girls and we looked all the better for it." She took out another cigarette, turning away from me, and lit it behind a cupped hand. Every time I'd ever seen the woman, she'd been minutes shy of lighting up. Her daughter's mother.

"He was stupid, though. He put his faith, his health, into the hands of men who didn't care about him like they said. Don't make that mistake, kiddo."

Up until this point, I'd been a man. Now she was talking to me like I didn't know anything and I sassed her for it. "It's easy to tell when someone doesn't like you. I'm not an idiot."

Her voice was almost a whisper, but urgent like the beating of a hummingbird's wing. She rested her hand gracelessly on my shoulder. "There's a difference between liking someone and caring about them, son. A lot of people are gonna *like* you, but only a few are gonna give a hoot about what happens to you.

"All of us girls had pictures of husbands and kids and grandkids, but all he had was a picture of a old dog—I never saw just how much sad there was in that until after he gone."

Wild onions grew between us and the mossy stone. A few blades of grass were taller than grave stone's peak, threatening to obscure it and us completely. A solitary hawk did doughnuts in the sky.

There was a sign at the gate asking for donations that would go towards a maintenance guy's hourly pay. I wondered what would happen if no one cared enough and all that grass, that kudzu, those weeds consumed it all.

It's what happens eventually, right? New people die and replace the old ones in importance. Everyone is forgotten and they hide your bones with red chert so that wild onions can grow and be all that's left of you.

I'd sleep better at night knowing that there was someone who cared enough to go around putting fresh, phony flowers on everyone's grave. It wouldn't matter if they were men dead from AIDs, women who'd abandoned their daughters, cruel older sisters, or feckless fifteen year old boys. In a perfect world, everyone would be respected and remembered in some capacity. Even dickwads.

I figured that's why my mother didn't sleep at all that night. With me down for the count, her chances at extended progeny were nil to none. Maybe she worried that she'd die and that no one would care enough to cut the grass on her grave in the summer or put out chrysanthemums in the fall. Or donate so that a maintenance guy could do it for them.

There was silence, save for the crickets and the breeze. There is no quiet like graveyard quiet.

"One thing I can say for Alabama is this. You go in the country far enough and all that separates you from the sun and the sky are a few power lines and the occasional church that has more money than it knows what to do with. It's beautiful here." She looked on me with eyes crowned by crow's feet.

"I know you're the type that'll get out of this place the first chance you get."

I was.

"Thing is, sometimes you'll catch yourself missing it. It sneaks up on you. Whether you know it or not, good things have happened to you here and there's no way of substituting them away. Alabama has a way of tricking me into thinking I'm a little girl again. Like I have choices to be made. When you're my age, there aren't as many options to choose."

"You're saying that it's too late for you to change your life even if you wanted?"

She looked doubtful. "I just don't know if it's worth the trouble. Getting older is hard work enough for me. Now I just want to fix my mistakes—not make new ones."

She offered her hand, gesturing for me to help her up, grunting like only a seventy year old woman who'd chain smoked for forty-seven could. I folded the blanket, tucking it into my armpit as she grappled for car keys in her smock pocket.

"Well, how does a late lunch sound?" She asked, patting herself down to shake loose any stowaway grasshoppers.

"Lunch would probably cost, what, six dollars for the both of us?" I asked.

"You don't worry about that. It's on me."

"No," I began, "it's not that. I just think I have a better idea. You know where there's a five and dime 'round here?"

At seventeen cents apiece, eighty clusters of fake flowers rang up to about fourteen U.S. dollars. We raided at least six consignment shops and two of them were across the Alabama state line. They took up her entire backseat and looked tacky as a church lady's crown, but I felt accomplished as we drove back to the graveyard. I said that I would pay her back someday.

"That money is gone like geese in high cotton and you know it. I'll never see it alive. It can go towards my own burial." She teased.

We were back at the graveyard just before four, and set to work. We tried to coordinate the flowers by color so that they didn't clash.

When we finished a while later, we met at the gate to survey our work. Hundreds upon hundreds of polyester blossoms plagued that cemetery; gaudy, unholy variations of every hue in the electromagnetic spectrum and a few colors that weren't. Some accented with glitter, beads and/or sequins. Tasteful old women would've needed smelling salts in abundance so as not to faint in horror.

She wiped a stroke of tar-black dirt from my chin, and her fingers were cold like a pewter belt buckle. I kept both hands firmly planted in front pockets, waiting for her to say how late it was getting, how she should get me home, and how my mother would worry.

I wanted to laugh. At fifteen, I was *just* young enough, just healthy enough and just strong enough, to double over and die myself.

"Want a cigarette?" she offered.

Post-Exorcism Lunchroom Fugue
Brandi George

It's the sea of students parting for me. They hold
        their crosses, but it's too late. The gold
has eaten all the branches from their halos.

                We live inside the air. We're folded
                dark matter, W.I.M.P.S..
                We move through you undetected.

It's my head crossing into metal, my head lost
        in the living room where a cat tosses
    its body into sunlit glass.

                We live inside birds. We're mammoths buried
                under basements, glaciers.
                We move through you undetected.

It's the scribbles on my face before school,
        the eye-shaped bruise
    on my chest, the oil crosses Cora drew

on the mirror, banishing me from the trapeze
        world. It's nowhere to eat my string cheese.

Poems Burnt In a Trash Barrel
Brandi George

I can't explain why people who do bad
are sometimes good, how their goodness
makes them weak, maybe drink too much,
sleep around or leave their young daughters

at home 24/7 with no one
to talk to, how those daughters might go crazy
and ask the living room: *Anyone there?*
When the daughter isn't answered at first,

she writes a spell to summon spirits,
and when that doesn't work, she puts on
a white dress, cuts herself while sitting
at the dinner table. She dances

to Insane Clown Posse and sneaks out, and sleeps
at the cemetery all in hopes
that her mother will come home and catch her.
So when the daughter leaves stacks of

angry poems on the counter the mother
reads them and calls the pastor, and the church elders
agree that the daughter couldn't have
written them because she's too young, a girl and—

*

Send your dreams
inward. Holograms flicker—
ghosts of my siblings. My
not-siblings. Sons

of ink and lyre.
Metal-workers
bright with their own sparks.

Birds shot in flight

remember what God
said: *His blood cries
to me.* Seven coins times
ten murdered

girls equals the radioactive
tree where we gather
eggs. Splinter
and sing for what is

unseen: albino,
holy, winged. In Death's temple,
I paint her sleeping
and awake—Eve (Eternal

Mother) equals a hand
on my breast,
books carved
from mountains.

*

The mother has nightmares
whenever angels burn her daughter's feet. They run
from fighter planes. The daughter drowns.
The mother is shot, willowy acrobat, scraping

her knee against the pavement. She drags
the daughter's pale corpse. How to explain
none of it was her fault. How
she is a sacred leaf.

There are beings inside and outside of time
that would love them, poems burnt in a duffle bag.
Dolls' princess gowns turn into black snakes in the fire.
If the daughter had taken off her shirt. If from the burning

letters her goddess, Shanara, rose
on adamantium wings. If The Undertow
cracked the farmhouse like an egg. If dragon fire,
pestilence, burnt crops, apotheosis into clouds.

I can't explain why people who do bad
are sometimes good. Her mother built her
a pink dollhouse trimmed with gold,
then wired it with electricity.

*

Fly letters. Fly ink. Fly
trees from the paper. Fly
Jesus. Fly, bonfire. Little poems, fly.

Driving Home From Choir Practice
Brandi George

I crashed my Grand Am into a ghost,
got out of the car and searched the tall grass.
I saw his blue eyes first.

> *Andromeda, o cricket*
> *Anthropomorphic thicket*
> *Throats of morphing birds*

I dialed my best
friend, then breathed into a plastic bag.
I crashed my Grand Am into a ghost

> *Hominids crawl*
> *Trailer halls*
> *Walls inherit holes*

a year after I prophesized my cousin's encephalitis
as a flood drowning him in his crib.
I saw his blue eyes first.

> *Lazuli serpent*
> *Lazarus spent*
> *His eyes persist*

Mother doesn't believe in psychiatrists,
only demons, so I can't confess:
I crashed my Grand Am into a ghost,

> *Car doors open*
> *Carrion doors*
> *Without hands*

and I need my fucking head checked. I crossed
my photos with oil when
I saw his blue eyes—

Armor of God
Amorous God
A morose God

the first step to getting rid of spirits.
My aunt wouldn't let me in her house after
I crashed my Grand Am into a ghost.
First, I blue his saw eye:

Air, o grant
Aerial graves
To my enemies

Deep Sea Fishing
Brenna Dixon

The oil would hit the Atlantic shore in two days, grey-black tar balls like obese tadpoles. That's what the news said, and it killed me, filled me with a dead sound because once that happened that was it, no one would want to be out there and I'd be homeless just like the scuba diver.

He puddled on my doormat in cracked yellow fins, a thinning surfer's mane drooping in his eyes and a paunchy beer gut pressing at his wetsuit. The guy's side was ragged against the backdrop of the Atlantic. I half-closed the door because crazies are a dime a dozen in South Florida.

"How'd you get here like that?" I asked.

He straightened all tall (which caused his wound to spurt a little blood) and said, "I'm freaking Poseidon and I'm outrunning the ocean." Dark blood welled through the fingers below his rib cage. His eyes narrowed. "I've been all up and down this damn building and you're the only one who opened the door."

My bad luck I guess.

It should be noted here that I'm on the 10th floor of a high-rise on Pompano Beach. The pink-orange one that looks like a dirty sunset. From my balcony I could see my fishing boats—Old Wilhelmina floating among the docks, The Good Lucille hunkered down on her trailer, shore-bound. Athena's weathered apartment building was several blocks west of my line of vision, but I still checked for it every day, just as I checked the waterline for the approaching oil spill.

When I didn't acknowledge that Poseidon had spoken, just stared at the bite beneath his ribs trying to figure out by radius which kind of shark got him, he snapped his fingers.

"You got any beer, man? I could really use a beer."

So I lit a smoke and invited him in for a Bud and some bandages. I figured it'd be bad karma to let some crazy dude with a god complex wander around the building until he passed out from blood loss.

Poseidon flipper-printed all down my carpet and onto the kitchen linoleum where he stood in front of the fridge playing with the hole in his side, fingers darting in and coming away bloody, then going back in to feel around some more. He rolled shredded bits of skin, or maybe wetsuit, between his fingertips. When he poked each piece back into his body, that was when my cigarette started tasting like dead fish. I stubbed it out in the sink, then brought in the gauze and ace bandage.

Poseidon popped the top on a can and sat at my kitchen table.

"Here," I said. I bent to wrap the gash and he snatched the materials away from me.

"I can do it myself," he said. He wound the bandages around and around his middle until the blood disappeared, never wincing.

"You can't stay long," I said. "I'm late for work. And why are you wearing a wetsuit?"

I threw a couple of dish towels over the pink water beneath him, and when he went to scratch, a piece of intestine or something fell out, rippling the puddle. I think he did it on purpose.

"You don't believe I'm me," he said.

"Poseidon?" I asked. "Not so much."

He stared hard in the direction of the sink, his skin concentrated in tight ripples between his eyebrows. I couldn't tell if he was sweating or if he was still wet from the ocean. His face grew redder, then finally slid back through shades of pink until he slumped down in his chair.

"Look in the sink, jerkwad," he said.

So I did.

My cigarette was gone. In its place: a sardine smushed face-first into the basin, its tail twitching in the air. I picked it up. Pressed its fleshy weight between my fingers. Its cool silvered skin. The lateral line horizontally spanning its body.

The 8 a.m. beer had nothing to do with it. The fish was legit.

I stared at Poseidon, thinking how much easier it would be to keep a fishing business afloat during an oil spill if I could just screw up my eyes and will the fish into existence.

"Give it here," he said, and beckoned with his fingers. I tossed the sardine over. He popped it in his mouth and swallowed. "Gotta refill the reserves."

I nodded. "Sure. Now tell me how you did that."

He took a swig of Bud.

"This is shitty beer," he said, squinting one blue eye at the can.

"Then have water," I said, sipping at my own.

Poseidon shuddered. He set his can down. "What's your name anyway?"

Nice of him to ask, right? Him coming into my house and getting blood on my floor and letting my beer dribble down his double chin?

"Donovan," I said. The name made me feel forty at ten years old and it still made me feel forty at thirty.

Poseidon crossed his legs and jiggled a flipper, flinging water around the kitchen. "Were you the kid who used to pop jellyfish and fill them with sand?" he asked.

I was. Their translucent skins stretched tight like sandwich bags, bulging with sea grit. Top-heavy. Thin, useless tentacles. I'd take them to the end of the pier and toss them, one by one, into the salty green water. Watching them sink was my favorite part. They disappeared in their hovering way.

"They were dead already," I said.

"Right, right," said Poseidon, running a hand through his hair, leaving behind red streaks. "Just making sure I have the right Donovan."

I didn't appreciate the way he said my name.

"You have to go," I said. "I have work." The tourists would be waiting, wanting to land the 400-pound marlin they'd heard about from a friend of a friend who'd once hooked one before it got away. No one hooked marlin anymore, but they didn't need to know that.

Poseidon stared at me, the creases in his tan face deepening. He looked old.

"Don't hang me out to dry, man," he said. "I can't go back in the water. Look. Let me level with you."

"You can level with me while we walk," I said. I checked my pockets for keys and headed out the door. Poseidon followed me into the elevator. The doors shut and for a good few seconds we stood there in complete silence, me watching him toy with the bandage plastered over his wound, him staring pointedly at the ceiling. The speakers in the elevator had broken months ago. No more muzak.

When the buzzer chimed for the eighth floor, Poseidon spoke.

"Leaving the water was a mistake, okay? You've made mistakes, too," he said.

"What do you mean I've made mistakes?" I asked. "You don't even know me."

I checked my watch. Athena got pissed when I was ten minutes late, let alone thirty.

Poseidon waved a hand. "You know. The whole oil rig thing. Before you went to college. When you were a roughneck."

I stopped. "How do you know about that?"

"Can we focus please? In case you haven't noticed, a shark attacked me."

He pointed to his side. The bleeding had slowed.

"So," I said. "People get attacked all the time. Only they don't usually survive."

"Sharks don't attack me."

"Why this one then?" I asked.

Poseidon glared at me. "Probably pissed about the oil spill same as everyone else."

"You can't fix it?" I asked.

"If I could, do you think I'd be dealing with this?" He pointed again to the bite in his side.

Despite losing what must have been gallons of blood, Poseidon hadn't gone into shock or died. Between that and the fish in my sink I figured there was at least some legitimacy to his god claim, which led me to a thought: seaweed dripping from his arms, an old bed sheet, a little plastic gold. The locals might not buy into it, but the Canadians—all those Ontario plates crowding the lots—they'd eat it up. And he could bring the fish. If he couldn't get rid of the oil, he could at least make it so no one walked away empty-handed. The spill would be here day after tomorrow. I needed as many fish as I could get.

We hit the first floor and stepped out of the elevator.

"I tell you what," I said. "You come work for me and you can stay in my spare room." I'd have to clear out the broken rods and old tackle boxes, but I'd been meaning to do that anyway.

For a minute I thought Poseidon was choking. His eyes even bugged out. I was a half-second from Heimliching him. Then he smiled a glinty sort of smile.

"I don't work for anyone," he said.

I smiled back. Entitlement. Everyone has a sense of entitlement these days, am I right? Every person on the boat deserves to catch a fish.

I swept an arm at the ocean. "Then go play king somewhere else."

He paled and I knew I had him. My meal ticket. My money man.

Poseidon bled slowly through the gauze and ace bandage wrapped around his side. He pulled at it while we walked down the sidewalk, a low stone wall between us and the sand, the sand between us and the ocean.

"Still looks pretty bad," I said.

"It'll heal over soon," said Poseidon. There was little conviction in his voice.

"Keep it covered or you'll freak out the customers," I told him.

Pavement heat seeped through the soles of my boat shoes. Poseidon thwacked along in his flippers, *slap slap slap*. Salt breeze rustled through palm fronds and sea grape leaves. Despite it all, despite my failing business—failing because during a recession no one has time for luxury, failing because nine times out of ten no one caught fish, failing because I couldn't afford to fix the outboard on The Good Lucille—I longed for open ocean. I longed for things to feel smaller.

Base camp for Don's Deep Sea Fishing was an old hot dog stand abandoned in a parking lot a few yards from the beach. Athena, my single employee and the woman I wanted more than anything, hated the salt-rusted tin roof. She said it made her edgy. I met Athena at Briny's Irish Pub when I first moved to Pompano eight years ago. She was the one behind the bar, hands full of glass and Guinness. When she laughed at my name and I asked hers, she shut right up. Then we both made our excuses—my parents walked down the aisle to "Mellow Yellow"; her parents felt her kick for the first time in Athens. When I needed a first mate, she was the only person to say yes to the job.

The day Poseidon entered the picture, Athena and I had two old women from Boca Raton signed up to catch dolphin. The fish, not the mammal. Only twelve customers in the past year had successfully landed dolphin.

The fishing shack's open rollaway hurricane shutters exposed Athena inside. She peered out of the darkness and fanned herself with a Mickey's Shrimp and Dogs take-out menu.

"A/C's broke," she said.

Fish-stink hung on the breeze.

"Blue-Hairs here yet?" I asked.

Athena paused, black curls sticking to her neck and chest, and glanced at Poseidon. Her tank top revealed the kelp tattooed up the inside of her left arm.

"Who's that?"

"Poseidon, Athena," I said. "Athena, Poseidon."

Poseidon's face went slack for a moment then rearranged itself into a smile.

I scratched my beard and peered out at the parking lot. The old purple beater we used to shuttle customers to the dock needed gas. Two or three fat, curly lizards sunned themselves on the electrical box that kept us in dim lights and, until then, air conditioning. Past that: People bunched along the pier railing. An old man in a Speedo exited the bathroom hut, rolls and rolls of stomach spilling over his tight, black suit.

No old ladies from Boca Raton.

"You know you just get hotter when you do that," I said, pointing to Athena's menu-fan.

"Do I?" She paused, eyes sleepy as if underwater, before turning to Poseidon. "What do you think?"

Then it happened. He turned on the god-charm. He squeezed his girth further into the stand, shoving me gut-first into the folding table, and took the fingers of the most beautiful woman on this shit strip of sand. He smelled her nail beds. Who does that? Who smells a person's nail beds? But Athena loved it, loved the way he compared her to tropical waters and living coral. I know this because her eyes narrowed and she smiled the kind of smile I'd only ever hoped she'd smile at me.

My face felt itchy with sweat and heat. I needed to shave.

"You exert more energy trying to keep yourself cool. You heat yourself up so the cooling effect cancels out," I said.

She didn't hear me. I could see her working to figure Poseidon out the way she figured out all of our clients. That's why she was so invaluable—she knew how to hook them in.

I shuffled through our dog-eared date book, looking for the Boca Blue-Hairs' appointment time.

"They say you beat heat with heat." I tossed her a warm water from under the desk. It knocked her in the chest, which I didn't mean for it to do, and she chucked it back at me.

"Jackass," she said.

I ducked and the bottle flew out onto the pavement, rolling till it hit sand. Maybe if I'd set up shop at the docks like all the other fishing outfits I wouldn't have been scrambling for loan payments. Except you had to have money to begin with to get a spot at the docks. Most of my roughnecking money had gone into my half-finished geography degree. The rest of it went into the boats. Athena resumed fanning herself and I motioned Poseidon outside where the air was cooler.

"Time to get dressed," I said.

Poseidon took the sheet and gaudy gold crown and raised an eyebrow. Blood trickled down his side.

"We'll grab some seaweed in a minute," I said. "Here." I shoved a broken spear gun at him. "Your trident."

"Nope," he said, and dropped it all right there in the parking lot. "No self-respecting son of Cronus would wear this shit."

I wanted a cigarette badly. I even went so far as to dig one out of my pocket and stick it between my lips before it turned into a sardine. After I spit it out, it lay there smoking on the pavement. We watched it, Poseidon and I, as it shriveled to an empty skin.

"Don't cross me," Poseidon said.

I pointed to the remnants of fish. "Do that out on the water, only bigger."

"You never said anything about going out there," he said.

"So don't go," I said. "I have work to do." I turned back toward the fishing shack, back toward Athena.

It wasn't fair the way Athena looked at Poseidon like he could do no wrong. I'd been working with her for two years and we'd only made out once, after christening The Good Lucille with a bottle of wine. Now it was all casual hip-bumps and her hand on my upper back as she slid past me in the small space we shared.

But despite all that, I needed Poseidon, needed him to bring the fish, so I walked slowly, hoping he wouldn't seriously leave.

Poseidon caught up to me. "Fine," he said, glancing at Athena. "But I'm staying in the wheelhouse."

She waved in our direction and we both waved back.

"No wheelhouse on my boat," I said.

A storm front hung dark and thick behind the lighthouse several miles down the coast. As the afternoon progressed the clouds crept steadily closer. Athena left every couple of hours and came back with Slurpees and Cokes from the 7-11 to keep us cool. Poseidon held each soda can with his fingertips.

"You're supposed to be outside getting customers," I said.

"Seriously, Don?" asked Athena. "It's about to pour."

Poseidon held out a hand.

"What?" I asked.

"Can I bum a cigarette?"

I stared at his cracked, green fingernails.

"Me too, while you're at it," said Athena.

"You don't smoke," I said. "You complain when I smoke."

She shrugged. "I'm trying new things."

Poseidon smiled a little and waggled his fingers. I dug two cigarettes out of my pocket and slapped them in his hand. He lit his, touched the burning end to the other, and handed it to Athena. She balanced the cigarette between her lips just as Poseidon had, her lips where his had been a second earlier. It was practically a kiss. The small space filled with smoke.

"I'm going to put gas in the van," I said.

"Wait. Don," said Athena. She coughed out a chestful of smoke and laughter. "Grab my gum out of the glove compartment?"

"Don't inhale so much," said Poseidon. He grinned. I stood and squeezed past him, making sure to bump his shark bite with my elbow.

"Not cool, man. Not cool," he said.

The air outside was thick with humidity, heavy with the oncoming storm, but it was fresh and god-free. I kicked at parking lot gravel and made my way to the old Windstar. Big, purple storm clouds hung over the far end of the pier. I sent up a quick prayer to whatever god ruled the sky. Please don't let it rain. Please don't let the oil roll in early. I scanned the water (nothing), then climbed in the driver's side and stuck my key in the ignition. Athena's loud, brash laughter echoed across the parking lot. I flipped off my own shop. Then I gave the ocean the bird, too.

I leaned out the window. "Take your sorry-ass god back," I shouted.

I turned the key. The engine sputtered and fell silent. A few fat, warm drops hissed on the pavement and smacked the windshield. No others followed. I slammed my palms against the steering wheel and the horn blared. I crossed the parking lot for the gas can only to find the shop window rolled down and locked.

A note taped to the door said: **DON. Biddies called. 8am tomorrow.**

Poseidon and Athena were gone.

At 5:00 P.M. my living room T.V. lit up with red and orange storm fronts and yellow ocean currents. Channel 6 said the tropical storm would hit full force by morning, bringing in the Gulf oil the morning after that. Nancy Nunez's toothy smile filled my screen.

"Watch your windows," she said. "Fill your bathtubs with water."

I dug my hurricane box out of the spare bedroom and dragged it into the living room. Candles, flashlights, canned food. I drank beer on my living room floor and balanced the business's books while I waited for Poseidon. Ten floors down, palm trees bent in the wind.

At 3 a.m. I woke up face-first in my budget book. The lights flickered, but stayed on. I peeled my cheek from the pages. Drool smeared the numbers of my **YOU'RE DOOMED** column into a bright red streak. Now I understood why Athena kept insisting I switch to a computer. A hard wind rattled my sliding glass door.

I dragged my feet over to the spare bedroom and stared at the empty futon in the far corner. I imagined Poseidon's hands on Athena's bare hips, Athena's chest against his chest. I forced myself to stop staring at the bed. Instead, I focused on the room. Broken poles leaned against the far wall. Four cracked buoys lay on the sagging futon. Boxes of who-knows-what—books maybe? old dishes?—spilled from the closet into the middle of the room. I closed the door.

In my own bedroom, I counted Mississippi's until I fell asleep.

My watch alarm went off at 7:15. I stumbled into the kitchen for a cup of coffee only to find Poseidon asleep on my couch, the ace bandage loose enough to show red flesh beneath. One arm dangled near the floor. I started a pot brewing then opened the blinds. A dark sky and heavy winds, but still no rain.

Poseidon groaned from the couch.

"That room's a shithole." He flung an arm in the direction of the spare room.

"How'd you get in?" I asked. I'd locked the door before going to bed.

"I'm a god, dumbass. I don't need a key." He smushed his face into the back of my couch. "Hey, thanks for locking me out by the way."

I poured myself a cup of coffee and hoped the throbbing between my eyes would go away. "Where's Athena?" I asked.

"How should I know? Is there coffee? I need coffee."

"You were with her, right? You guys left the shop together?" My stomach clenched.

"I don't know, man. Yeah, I was with her, but I guess she's at home, okay?" Poseidon sat up. "What time is it?"

"Just after 7," I said. "What'd you guys do last night anyway?"

Poseidon grinned. "What do you think?" He stood and stretched, wincing at the tightness of his scabbing shark bite.

Bile rose in my throat. "Be ready to go in ten."

"Have you looked outside?"

"Yeah. Not much time to catch fish before the oil hits, right?"

I closed my bedroom door and called Athena. She didn't pick up.

Poseidon groaned about his head the whole walk to work.

"Shut up," I said. "It's like you've never had a hangover before."

"Gods are immune," he said.

"Obviously not."

We found Athena slumped in front of the shop, head resting on her knees. She looked up at us, bleary-eyed, as we approached.

"Took you guys long enough," she said.

"Are you okay?" I asked.

She tied her hair up in a messy bun and stood. "I'm fine. You, on the other hand," she pointed to Poseidon, "are a grade-A asshole and I hope you die."

I grinned and opened the door.

"What happened to your key?" I asked.

Athena rolled up the hurricane shutter.

"Ask him," she said, jabbing a finger in Poseidon's direction.

Poseidon put an arm around Athena's middle. "Come on," he said. "We had fun, right?"

Athena backhanded him in the side, right in the shark bite. Poseidon turned a pale shade of green. I handed over his god garb.

"I thought I told you I'm not wearing this," he said.

"Put it on," said Athena.

He stalked outside. "This is shark weather, you know," he shouted.

Through the open shutter: the ocean, slate grey and rough. Looked like rain soon. Athena traced her tattoo and stared vacantly at the far wall.

At 8:00 on the dot our two old biddies crossed the parking lot and stopped in front of our stand. Gucci Glasses touched her hair and said to Botox, "D'you think this is it?"

"Mrs. Horowitz?" I asked. Neither of them seemed to hear me.

"Eileen Horowitz?" I tried again.

Botox dug around in her purse for something and I wondered if they were both blind and deaf. I imagined Poseidon poking them with the trident he refused to hold.

"Hey lady!" shouted Athena. The biddies snapped to.

"You don't need to shout," said Botox. "We were just looking for our coupon."

Both women spoke with a heavy New York accent.

"Your coupon?" I asked.

"Yes," said Botox. "The one from the newspaper."

I hated myself for those stupid vouchers. *Two-For-One Fishing! Don's Deep Sea Fishing!* It'd been a last-ditch effort to get summer customers. The result? Twice as many unhappy fishless customers.

Botox slid a rumpled piece of newspaper across the counter along with her ID: Eileen Horowitz. Athena handed Eileen's license back and checked Gucci Glasses' (Gail Leibowitz).

I made a mental note:

Botox = Eileen

Gucci Glasses = Gail

Eileen and Gail.

"Alright, ladies," Athena said. "Are you ready to set sail?"

The old ladies squeezed under the overhang and peered at the sky.

"Do the fish bite in the rain?" Eileen asked. "It looks like rain."

Poseidon peeked his head around the corner. "Yes."

"Who are you?" asked Gail. "Are you the captain?"

"No, I'm the captain," I said.

"Then who's he?"

Poseidon shot a glance at Athena, held a finger up at the ladies, and disappeared behind the shack. He emerged in full-sheeted get-up and endured the ensuing flash photography.

"I'm Poseidon," he said. The ladies laughed.

Athena scowled. "Let's go," she said. "Right this way, ladies." She headed toward the van.

"Trust me," she whispered loudly. "He's no god."

I filled the van's tank with the gas can, then ushered everyone over, hoping the rain would hold off for a couple more hours.

Athena loaded fly rods and tackle into the back, then climbed in the passenger side door and left Poseidon to the old ladies. We pulled out of the parking lot and she glared at the road ahead.

"Your eyes are glassy," I said. "You okay?"

"I'm fine," she said. "And my eyes aren't glassy." She rubbed her eyes. "Lucille's engine is still shot, right?"

"Yeah."

"Fly fishing will be interesting on Wilhelmina," she said.

Behind us, Gail and Eileen talked over Poseidon, ignoring him entirely. Apparently Gail was going through a late-in-life divorce and Eileen thought it would be good for her to get out on the water for a few hours. Poseidon leaned past them and kissed Athena's shoulder. She shoved him back into his seat. Hard.

◆

Old Wilhelmina's a twenty-eight foot center console, a little water-stained, but otherwise clean. It took a couple turns to get the outboard running, and I prayed the whole time that it wouldn't die on me. In the end we made it out to sea, Poseidon in his sheet, Athena with those legs of hers, the old biddies in their hats and life vests, and me in an old Guy Harvey shirt. I handed everyone rain ponchos. At least Poseidon looked stupider than I did, but damn if he didn't try to own that sheet. He stood hands on hips so that it hid his belly. The shark bite wasn't bleeding through the new gauze yet, so I could almost imagine what he must've looked like before the shark went after him.

Water sloughed off Wilhelmina's sides, curling behind her, frothy against the grey water. The wind buffeted us from side to side. I adjusted left, then right, then left to keep us on course. Poseidon sat dead center in the boat, head between his knees, muttering something or other to himself. Then there it was: a floating mass of dead palm fronds and old wood. A fruitful blemish on the great face of the ocean. Here's where we'd find dolphin. Since Gail and Eileen were two-for-one I hoped that here was where we'd get tip money, where they'd decide that *the girls* just *had* to come out on the water because what an *experience*.

Athena came down from the helm, bumping Poseidon on her way to gear up Eileen and Gail.

"For commander of the seven seas, you sure are being a wuss," she said.

She was right. Every time the boat rocked he clutched the spear gun tighter, ducked his head lower, until finally Eileen stepped over and laid a hand on his shoulder.

"My Hubert used to get the sea sickness. Do you have the sea sickness? I have some Dramamine in my bag. Let me give you some Dramamine."

Poseidon raised his face, drawn and sad. Eileen cupped his cheek, ran a hand through his hair, murmured something about Hubert again.

"Can I talk to you for a minute?" I nodded toward the console and Eileen offered Poseidon a hand to help him up. He stood hunched and shaky. The wind wrapped his god sheet tight around his body.

"What?" he asked. I noticed he was breathing a little hard, and I felt sort of bad, but the oil would be here tomorrow morning, would suffocate the fish and kill my business.

"Look," I said. "Can you get these people some fish?" And here I got an idea. "Maybe if we use a net we can catch a ton of them and save them and set up a pond or something, you know? So when the ocean can't be fished at least our pond can."

Sweat broke out at the backs of my knees. Poseidon watched as Athena showed Gail how to cast.

"Keep the wrist straight," she said. "Ten and two."

"If you can't, that's fine. But Athena..."

Black clouds filled the sky. I dug five lifejackets out of the empty livewell and handed one to Poseidon. He dropped it on deck.

"Are you serious, man? Of course I can get fish. But you'll never keep them alive in a pond," said Poseidon. He kicked the lifejacket, disgusted and righteous and god-like.

He sat in the console chair and closed his eyes, rubbed his fingers together, cracked each knuckle. His face grew red and he began to sweat.

Seagulls wheeled above us, white against the dark sky.

"Just give me a second," he said.

Trembling, Poseidon rose and walked to the side of the boat, steeling himself against the bigger waves the way a surfer might—wide stance, palms down. He lay on his stomach and slipped his arms beneath the railing until his fingers trailed in the water. And for a while he stayed like that.

When Eileen came over with the Dramamine, her eyes went wide.

"Oh my God," she said. "His side."

Poseidon's blood dripped, drop after drop, on deck. Next to him, Gail doubled over with a fish on her line. We use fly rods when we want customers to feel the fight more. Fly rods make fish feel bigger. Since dolphin school near the surface, we thought, hell, give the ladies a show if the fish'll bite.

"Jackson would love this," Gail whispered. I'm guessing Jackson was her soon-to-be-ex husband.

She gripped her pole so tight all ten knuckles went white. She squared her stance, leaned back against the weight of the fish and reeled. The line screamed.

"Check the drag," I said. I hurried over to her, imagining the line snapping, imagining an impossible marlin getting away. Gail's brow scrunched with concentration, her eyes sharp and bright.

"Got him," she breathed.

She pulled back and the fish jumped, a bright spot of green and blue against all the grey. A dolphin. It smacked back against the surface and the line went slack.

"Reel in slowly," I said.

The line went tight again as the fish dove. The rod tip bent toward the surface.

"He's going under the boat," I said. "Pull up, pull up."

But the rod only had so much give and Gail leaned far over the railing, then there she went, a pale streak of varicose veins and sun block dropping over the edge, sinking like one of the sand-heavy jellyfish of my childhood. I had to give her credit for holding onto the rod. Most first-timers would've let go.

Thunder left my ears ringing.

We all froze on deck.

"Shit," whispered Athena.

Eileen's scream kicked her into action, and Athena shoved me into movement.

"Get Gail," she said.

"Gail!" Eileen screamed. She peered over the edge, searching for her friend. Poseidon sat slumped and bleeding against the railing.

Athena sprinted to him and I sprinted starboard, leaning as far over the water as I could, trying to grasp hold of Gail's hand. She was too far below the surface.

So I jumped.

Cold, dark water billowed through my shirt, buoying me, inflating my shorts. My shoes slipped off, and my hat. Water moved like fingers through my hair, scraped through my beard. I swear the water spoke to me and I closed my eyes and listened. Footsteps from the boat. Are we really that loud? I wondered. Can shoes make so much noise? No wonder no one catches fish anymore. Fish. I opened my eyes and there was Gail being pulled along by her fishing rod. She'd lost a shoe and it floated past my head as I groped my way through the water, clawed my way toward her. Salt stung my eyes and I reached for her, squinted to see what was pulling her slim body down down down. There was no bottom, no surface, only ocean. Only me and Gail and the quiet. I remembered what Poseidon had said about this being shark weather and goosebumps popped up on my skin.

I pumped my arms, kicked my legs, made my muscles burn. I touched her ankle, cool and thin and fragile. She turned to me, gave me a thumbs-up and an empty smile. She'd lost her dentures. And then her body dispersed. She became so many bubbles and I was left clutching nothing but my own thumb. The fly rod drifted deeper and deeper and gone.

Rain battered the surface above me. I kicked. I broke through to air. I breathed and breathed and breathed. Then I looked. Then I saw the blood.

"Don!" Athena shouted. "Donovan!"

Her arms were covered. Deep red trickled over Wilhelmina's sides and I swam through the murk, trying not to think of platelets, trying not to think of sharks. Eileen pulled me up, though I don't know how.

"Where is she?" Eileen asked. "Gail."

I slumped on deck. Drops of rain fell from her nose.

"I don't know," I said.

Her face crumpled. She swiped a hand over her face then pointed a finger at me.

"Get a good lawyer," she said.

Then she stepped through the blood to Poseidon.

His chest heaved. Someone had taken off the sheet and there he was in his wetsuit and flippers, black and yellow in all that red. Athena hugged me and even in all this mess I loved the feel of her breasts against me.

"You're okay," she said.

She sat at Poseidon's head, doing her best to keep the blood out of his hair. His side burbled and my stomach turned. I'm not proud of it, but I puked over the side.

"It was a bull shark," Poseidon said. I knelt next to him, pressed my hands to his waist.

"One of my favorites," he said. "They eat damn near everything, can live in salt water, brackish water, fresh water."

Eileen gripped the railing, looking out toward nothing.

The boat rocked and lightning arced the sky.

"What happened to Gail?" I asked. "Where'd she go?"

Athena came back with two towels grimy with bait and dried fish slime. They didn't last long against Poseidon's bite.

"Who knows, man?" he said.

"What do you mean you don't know? Aren't you supposed to know?"

My temples throbbed. A lost customer; no landed fish; an imminent oil spill. My business was over. Done. Gone.

Poseidon laughed. "Shit just happens." There was blood in his teeth.

He ran his fingers down his side. The bite was ragged and writhing, like the flesh was trying to knit itself back together.

We'd gone about a hundred feet before the outboard quit. The flare sputtered out three feet above the water. Mostly we kept the flashlight off. Why bother wasting battery when we knew what was around us? Four different sets of breathing: Eileen's, soft and shuddery; Athena's, decisive, intentional; Poseidon's, long and wet; my own, a hollow sound in my ears. Bits of driftwood smacked against Wilhelmina's sides; palm fronds scraped her hull. Waves washed the deck clean of blood.

After a while we grew used to the sounds, we grew sensitive to subtle changes, so when Eileen swore the water sounded heavier, I turned the flashlight on and held it over the side. Dark water, but water's always dark before daylight hits. Another wave washed over us, streaking the deck brown.

"Is that oil?" asked Eileen. "Oh my God, that's oil."

By late morning, tar balls would wash ashore, beach-goers would be horrified, would then get over their horror and move on to golfing or air boating or bargain-hunting. They'd build new theme parks to house the tourists. My eyes burned and I turned so Athena wouldn't see.

Her hand on my shoulder. Her cheek on my neck, cool on my sunburn. The flashlight beam swung. Tiny glints of orange and red, hundreds of pelicans floating around us, soaking from brown to black.

"Damn it," Poseidon breathed. "Fine. I'm coming."

"Who are you talking to?" I asked.

A shuffle, then a splash. A small "oh" from Eileen.

In the beam of the flashlight we saw him sink, saw the bull shark come for him. The water thrashed then bubbled then went still. Sunrise came at 5:45 a.m. Around six, a battered party yacht towed us to shore where the water was still clean. *The Neptune*, it was called. They'd been stuck out in the storm, too, and wanted to see the fish we'd butchered to get ourselves so bloody.

"Must've been marlin, eh?" said one balding man. He flashed us a grin. "A little on-deck sushi?"

"Dolphin," said Eileen. She didn't bother clarifying. I think she enjoyed their horror.

Illustration by Stephen Smith

We scanned our wake for signs of Gail the whole way back.

I still get a Christmas card every year from Eileen addressed to Don's Deep Sea Fishing even though her lawyer put me out of business. The card always has some rendition of Poseidon on the front. This year he wore a Santa hat. Last year he drove a sleigh led by seals.

Athena and I make ends meet. Disaster tours bus through to see the oil slick now, to watch the waves roll in black and streak back to the sandy edges. We sell the tourists lemonade and listen to the bus drivers blare statistics through their megaphones.

"Florida's coastal activities once generated $13,035,087,800," they say. "Not so much anymore, folks. Not so much anymore."

While the tourists take pictures of tar balls, laugh at their black feet, buy cheap magnets and salt and pepper shakers from the tourist shops, Athena and I see to Old Wilhelmina. The oil still won't come off. We've tried everything. When passersby ask about the other stains, the redder ones, we tell them nevermind those. And when they keep at us to answer, we tell them she once carried a god.

Night Jetty
Hastings Hensel

Still when we sleep the sleek
spindrift-pitched
rock jetty lifts the salt-spray,

prints white the black night
a madness—this
that, nonetheless without us,

persists. But it's not exactly
the loneliness
the fish possess, finning past

what seem like giant's teeth,
high tide-sheathed,
some Jurassic spine reclined,

deepening the dark channel
where they swim,
as far away and quiet as stars.

Conversion Narrative in a Walk-In Freezer
Hastings Hensel

I staggered, bourbon-haggard, inside,
hoping to sober up as the door swung

shut. Outside, the other men gathered
around their laughter as if it were fire.

Frigid crypt of field-dressed, headless,
gutted bucks with back-straps stripped,

each hooked and strung up like Christ,
haunches hanging over nauseous me.

I slid down, shivered, spun and woke
suspended by my belt on a meat-hook,

at a height where each white underbelly
I now saw as a field stiffened with snow,

and, below, each antler a leaf-stripped
winter tree, a river-worn eye of stone.

There I came to, knew, bare-bone chill,
as outside, with laughter, men burned.

Snag Arrangement
Hastings Hensel

Everything ornamental and forlorn:
plugs hung up in the limb-clutch,
plastic worms wrapped around
and squirming from the power-lines,
spinner-baits stuck in the stumps.
Everything snatched up: foul-hooks
by snot-grass clumps and mud-sunk
brush piles, jigs in the oyster beds.

Everything fragmented, faithless:
never the fish one wished for more
than God. Everything suspended
in the upside down—miscast as if
one mistook a clear sky for water
and went out fishing for the birds.

Widowmaker
Hastings Hensel

Stump the high tide hides,
driftwood the floods bring—

the river fisherman's kenning
for when he comes screaming

down the one river he's known
longer than his own signature.

Dark, unseen. Like a thought
I should have further explained.

Let me explain: I am terrified of
always weaving between things,

trying to gauge my lust purely,
the timing and depth, the man

whose arms surface, reach out
of the blue to you, after my death.

Bycatch
Hastings Hensel

Not the almighty succulent shrimp
hand-picked like jewels from the pile
hauled in and dumped by the trawl,

nor even the clichéd rubber boot,
nor the terrified and pathetic dolphin.
Not Ophelia in her muddy dress,

her mouth forever opened in song,
yet still it meant money: *square grouper*,
the deck crew coined their bycatch

when they withdrew from the ocean
two fifty-five-gallon drums of cocaine.
But even then no long moral debate,

nor any predicament about what to do.
This was it: an exit from the stench-work
of fish guts and salt-covered waders,

seagulls forever screaming behind them
like a requiem for lives of prosperity.
So the crew sold it all summer and waded

in the money. *We know what we are but
know not what we be*, Ophelia mumbled
before her leap into the river, and who

among them thought they'd be caught
like shrimp or dolphin or rubber boots
in the profiteering nets of the law?

Periscope (Hart Crane)
Lauren Eyler

L.,

    A small one-bedroom house with a foyer, a bathroom and a courtyard. I have called out *is anyone here* and received no reply. My voice does not echo, even if I try to imagine it doing so.

    You would wish me to continue the description of this Zone, of this small one-bedroom house with a foyer, a bathroom and a courtyard. You have never been inside a government-sanctioned area where an individual is allowed, on his/her fourth day of residence, to commit the act of Selbstmord. Why should I evade the listing of nouns with preceding adjectives to describe the room that I sleep in? After all, the government will mail anything that I write and address.

    You, like myself, have read descriptions of various Rehabilitation Zones in the Papers. You have photographs that you can pick up and study and place me in. So many have pointed out that description can never be an exact replication. A statement like *there are three guns resting atop a blue cooler filled with German liquor* can be seen in infinite ways. Even if I were to go into the minutia, you could never imagine even a bullet, the way it takes shape in the house or the way its existence forces the house to mold to it. I am sorry if I have disappointed you.

    And after I had finished the description of the Zone that I have refused you, you would want to know how I lived out the three days before I made my decision. I must have wandered around the house or paced or lumbered or shuffled or pranced. I could have listened to music, clocks ticking, records of whales' songs. I could have smelled eucalyptus, wet dogs, aloe. Perhaps, I lay in the bed on sheets that felt the same as my mother's touch.

    Most of all you want to know why I did it, why I decided to carry this or that out. What does a person you love think before performing a voluntary murder of the self? Again, you can open the Papers and read the various rationalizations like we did as children.

    We played, while poring over these letters, Thumbs Up and Thumbs Down. We created seven categories: had become a burden to family/friends, philosophical musing, had exhausted all the reasons to live, boredom, belief that one is a failure, unrequited love and illness, whether physical or mental. After reading each letter, we tore it out of the magazine and placed it in the folder labeled with the reason. Boredom, philosophy, exhaustion and illness received a thumbs up. On the rest, we wrote arguments against the writer's perception.

    The look on my mother's face when she found them beneath my bed. She forced me to burn them one by one. I placed them in the oven until they withered into a gold that soaked the print from the paper. This is why I no longer wanted to play.

Then, I could not admit to you that I had been foolish enough to hide our work in such an obvious place. Moreover, there was a feeling of loss. I would never be able to read them again. In those moments, when desolation overwhelmed me, I would go to the library with a pen and paper and try to recount some of my favorites. I knew I could never do them justice, but, nonetheless, I spent hours in my attempts to reproduce them. When finished I would wad up my musings, lest my mother should find them, and throw them in the garbage before I left.

Later, in a college art class, I was to be reunited with the genre. My professor handed out bits of letters that described the interiors of various Zones and ordered us to create a rendition of what was described. Unfortunately, at that time, I was a realist. My paintings lacked imagination, but, now, I believe that my realist period led me to my current abstract ways. Thankfully, I had a professor that was willing to indulge me.

How does a dilettante begin an artistic practice: by imagining that they are worthy of doing so. With the letters we read, with the letters I'd written engraved in my blood, I picked up a paintbrush and palette and began to place reality on the page. With the truth of the world embedded in my mind, I felt competent in rendering these scenes.

I cannot recreate the paintings with words. I cannot reproduce colors on a page. I go as far as saying I created a color that looked like that of single malt whiskey, or going farther, still I could say that the end result was more the color of a single malt whiskey's residue. What does that mean? Again, I see the same problem of the bullets arising. This makes me too tired. I can search high and low, but I will never make you understand the color of single malt whiskey. And if I were to place a myriad of colors on the page with such specificity, your mind would run over them and only see what you wanted. You wouldn't take the time to consider Grand Hotel Awning, Lost Atlantis, Roasted Pine. For that matter, if I were in your place, neither would I.

The paintings no longer exist. They were a cycle of three, one painted atop the other. Although I won't discuss my composition, I will leave the pieces of the letters that I memorized to assist in my artistic endeavors. Perhaps this is the last gift I can give you, the words of others.

◆

They let me in here and took all my smokes. Not one in the bastard house and they knew I was a smoker. Out in the courtyard I dug holes. Hole after hole. Not one goddamn cigarette. I've got twelve hours left until I can pull the trigger. But fuck me. Where's my last request?

Then there's these guys. Two days ago they just showed up out of no-where. Four guys, on bikes. They were wearing these goofy goggles that went back to god knows how long. Their shirts said JB and Louvet. All of 'em were smoking. When one of 'em finished a cigarette, one of his pals would light him another. Once the cigarette was lit and in place, the guy with the new cigarette would say Merci, Merci

Illustration by Stephen Smith

I thought these guys would help me out if I said s'il vous plait so I walked over and started repeating it and they kept saying thank you, thank you and me please, please. No one of 'em stopped, so I threw myself at 'em and slammed into an invisible wall. I smashed into the pavement, but I kept at it. Not one of 'em slowed down.

Now I can't drink the gin and tonics in my room. I can't drink them without cigarettes. I'm bloody, bleeding on the sheets, the concrete porch ripped me up. I look out the window of my room and see those guys pedaling with their cigarettes and infinite thank yous and damn it. DAMN IT. I know laying here that it's the only thing I'll see out of any of the windows. They come and don't go.

◆

You know I came to get away from your alligators. Anywhere there is water in the house you have planted their eggs. Four beady eyes in the toilet bowls. One full-grown in the bathtub. It was the coffee pot that drove me to this place. Every morning I'd go to make coffee. Every morning I'd find eggs in the pot. I'd watch them while they broke their shells with their egg teeth. For a while, I could watch because I love you. Then, the days came when I couldn't.

During those days, I dreamt of caffeine. I dreamt of cold showers for heat rash. I dreamt of unoccupied water glasses or an empty ice cube tray. You managed to turn even the trays into swamps.

By that point, I couldn't drink anything anymore. I avoided the refrigerator at work. I shoved my cart past the rows of liquid at the grocery store. Water fountains were things to fear. The pipes in the walls, in the ceilings could burst.

When I arrived at the RZ, I wasn't afraid. In a note on the table, they assured me that the house was alligator free. They said drink and I did.

They'd stocked the house with coffee pots, ice trays and bathtubs. I drank water cooled by ice. I haven't done this since I moved in with you. I haven't touched water. I have not swallowed water. I was surprised in all that time that I still had tears to cry and I wasted the water I had to spill on you.

After drinking my fill of water, after rubbing ice cubes down my arms to my hands, down my legs to my knees, I went outside. An Olympic-sized pool. Over our two years together, I'd forgotten about swimming pools. I'd forgotten my trip to the Olympic trials. I'd misplaced my bronze medal in the move. When I remembered these things, I thanked them for putting the pool here. I said a little prayer to them.

It was the same pool from Barcelona. The lanes sectioned off by metal with buoyant pieces of plastic, red, yellow, blue. But in the lanes, I saw the bumps, the cretinous scabs, the arch that surrounded their heinous eyes.

The alligators are doing laps. I've been sitting here for ten minutes and they've completed two. All of the lanes are occupied. I hope they die from the chlorine before they kill me.

◆

I know I've seen them on TV. The host raises the authors from the dead. The authors kill themselves all over again. Well here, it's a live action show that never stops.

Hart Crane jumps into the ocean saying "Goodbye, everybody." Along side him, John Berrymen hits the west bank of the Mississippi and drowns in mud. David Foster Wallace strings himself up. Kane joins him. Plath opens the oven. Sexton starts her car. Hemingway shoots his favorite shotgun.

There is beauty. They go all at once, they jump, swing, slit, asphyxiate and they do it again and again and again, but I am wasting time with this. I am wasting the novel. This is just a letter. It is addressed to no one. It will go where I go wherever that is.

◆

An egg tooth, Sexton's suicide, bicyclers say thank you. But, you won't see those paintings now. I slashed the canvas and moved on. I recognized the need to paint the magical: patio furniture, trees, Jesus on the cross. You can imagine all of these things. The strength of magic, an exhale into the cold.

I know I have left you wanting. You will crawl in and out of the Kübler-Ross model. You are howling and demanding me to start over, redraft, add this and that and perhaps take something or another out. Make it clear. Be kind to you. Give you access to my motivation. You want me to say it's not your fault, but you wouldn't believe me. Either way you'll sit with your lips stuck to a martini glass and drown yourself every day. Or maybe that's projection, writing what I would have done. What I did do when my wife died. I don't know. You've been watching all this time since the day of her funeral.

You want me to conjure the Christ Jesus as you have been doing for so many years. You want me to imagine that he can save me. But, by now, this is an unnecessary wish. I am already dead. Take comfort that you can still imagine and demand.

This is the last bit of palaver that I have for you. Where is this going? Why did I write you nothing and throw in pieces of stories that DO NOT belong to me. I can sleep a bit easier tonight because I know that when you see an alligator swimming in the public pools, or bicyclers or cigarettes or a rerun of the suicide mini-series, or come across a Sexton poem you will not see those things. You will see only me. The signified.

Yours,

E.

How the Moose Fell in Snow
Donald Illich

You said something,
then I said something.
You wanted to talk
about moose, their habitat,
how you hunted them,
what their antlers looked like.
I wished to discuss
eternity, its nature, how
everything might not last
that long, how you and I
had souls, maybe eternal.
You changed the subject
to snack cakes, types
and sweetness, how
they were addictive,
how you dreamed of them,
how they made your wife
upset. I remarked
about death: who is he,
why is he cutting us down,
how can we beat him
and live forever and ever?
I mentioned to you
how the moose fell in snow,
blood on their heads.
How your cakes couldn't
bribe the Reaper.
You turned around and left.
It was a foul, overcast day.
In conditions like these,
we could choose
to believe in anything.

The Real Thing: My Life in Coke
Deborah Gold

When I was ten, I would sit on the floor in front of the television, winking at the door-length mirror angled towards me. Wearing periwinkle Danskin elastic-waist shorts and a striped sleeveless top, I hugged my bare knees to my chest, tilted my head like Agent 99, and watched myself kiss my kneecaps–chewily, the way the stewardesses of *Love, American Style* kissed their weekly dates. This was done to the harmonies of "I'd Like to Teach the Word to Sing"–the infamous Coke anthem, in which gauze-smocked hippies from around the small world stood circled atop a sunset hill, singing, swaying, and tipping icy, dark bottles to their lips. It was a jingle that evolved into a real song, somehow, and was the only piano number, besides the intro to "Mrs. Robinson," that I regularly practiced.

I kissed and re-tilted, one eye squinting up to analyze my style in the mirror, even though this destroyed the illusion of the kissee: the orange-haired Ned Van Meter, who could burp like a bullfrog and was nerdy enough to be my first real romantic possibility. Unlike the softball players with their monkey-headed buzz cuts, or the feverishly pink-cheeked Edwin, long-lashed and fragile, Ned was the class science brain, but he could also be as silly and giddy as me. If *Monty Python* had existed then, we'd have been swapping dead-parrot jokes, but instead I was charmed simply by his deep-throated *ribbets*. And when his Toad-style glasses were replaced with thin gold frames, he dazzled with his hair and freckles and ability to focus a microscope to reveal the scooting one-celled paramecia our class had grown in jars of water-soaked straw.

I'd like to buy the world a Coke, and keep it company.
The sun glowed on that TV hilltop–it was obvious even in black and white. The teenagers swooned and swayed, passing Coke bottles down the line. "I'm going to marry you, Ned," I declared. This was sacred: he was only the second boy I'd sworn that to after my dog.

They called it "The Hilltop Commercial," and it went down in advertising history, although for years, I had no idea anyone else treasured it besides a few other '70s piano/organ students and me. Coke might as well have been a martini for all I was allowed to drink it at that age, but I was hooked on the dream of communal love, and, somewhere down the line, world peace.

My balloon popped a month later, upon seeing Ned curled up in tears, the glasses punched from his face. He was lying on the floor, hands clamped between the knees of his black shorts, the buzz-cut boys having kicked him in the crotch, a cruel fact of male life previously unknown to me. His halo of desirability–and my compassion–fizzled. The paramecia jar in his hand had slipped and shattered, stinking up the room with a brackish smell that lasted weeks.

Before long, my girlfriends and I started kissing pillows for group critique and stretching shirts over our knees to see how we'd look as giant-boobed Playboy Bunnies. But for those private nights in front of the mirror, the Real Thing was all golden promise. Only later, when I could sneak a cup at a birthday party or temple *Oneg Shabbat*, would the actual Coke turn out to have a rusty tang, sinus-stinging fizz, and a taste only sickly-sweet.

◆

Like Fritos, Barbies, Christmas caroling, marshmallow-topped desserts, straight hair, training bras, Ouija boards, navy windbreakers, clackers (which actually could knock someone's brain out), spray shampoo, and Wonder Bread...like all those all-American things, for me Coke remained out of reach. With my mother a late-1950s British emigre and my father a third-generation Jewish New Yorker, we didn't fit anywhere, much less in the not-quite-New South of the 1970s, but the real drag was that my parents would not even let us try. While they celebrated their triumph in breaking a restrictive covenant barring Jews from the cul-de-sac, the real magic spells of assimilation—the miracle of stacked Pringles or Easter eggs with mallow whites, the enchanted promise of vanity sets and Dressy Tressy dolls, and later the casual hook of a bra, the snap of a pair of velveteen Viceroys, and the aerosol spray of deodorant in gym class—were necessities invisible to my parents, if not scorned outright. Yet all I needed was the right combination of power objects to spark my alchemical change into someone who belonged: if Plastigoop could be transmuted into something as delightful as Incredible Edibles, then surely so could I.

So when my dad began offering me two quarters for the temple Coke machine, pre-teen Hebrew School became a little more worthwhile. Especially since I had no choice about going.

◆

They weren't messing around when they put a Coke machine in the synagogue's Hebrew School hallways. Someone knew that it would take more than the Lord our God, parents, and a nonexistent thirst for spiritual knowledge to keep kids coming back—and while we weren't allowed to use it around Saturday youth services, so weighted with their relevance, halting guitar, and Beatles songs ("see, the Fool on the Hill is actually Moses..." and nobody was even stoned), the machine was fair game for Sundays and Hebrew School on Tuesday-Thursday afternoons.

Ani holaich al bet ha-safer—I go to school/the house of the book—is the only thing I still remember, along with *Sheket bevakashah!*—be quiet—the number one Hebrew school phrase since the time of the sages. Bar/Bat Mitzvah class began after regular Sunday School was done: in the sanctuary upstairs, the eternal light beamed on and the cushioned chairs were all flipped shut; the classroom wing was dark and empty, lit only by the promising glare of the Coke machine, which shook the floor tiles with its hum. I sat near the back of the classroom full of 12-year-olds on the brink of "manhood" and "young womanhood," terms intoned in vain as the folded paper footballs and *kippah* frisbees flew. Those too slack to learn the dot-notes to sing their Bar Mitzvah haftorah portions carried cassette recordings of the Hebrew School principal singing them, or even worse, stumbled through English transliterations; between debating the lifeboat dilemmas of our "Still, Small Voice" textbook, we listened endlessly to these chanted recitations. The classroom itself smelled of wax polish and rust, and somehow the smell became the taste, making the machine Coke brought back from break time always disappointingly flat and sour. But given my two quarters, each week I hoped for the best.

We'd moved across the county since joining this synagogue, and naturally the burden of driving fell to my mother, the non-believer, and only occasionally to my dad, who always made us so late that the reproving glares were not worth the insistence that he drive us. By the year Bar Mitzvah class came around, though, there was a kid, Zack Goldstein, from my own junior high to carpool with, and on this particular rainy morning, I'd ridden with Zack and his dad. A curly-haired wise guy, Zack was short and gremlin-like, with a perpetual Alfred E. Neuman grin. I was even further down the real school popularity scale, so outside of these car rides, we pretended not to know each other.

◆

A hard March rain was falling and the Goldsteins' cramped car had been steaming. Sunday School had been routinely tedious, full of "modern" Hebrew practice dialogues about movies, bus stops, and television, meant to assure us that life in the Promised Land was every bit as convenient as it was here, aside from having a few thousand trees to plant and wars to fight with unpredictable regularity. And, hey, Eretz Israel might be a desert, but it was groovy enough to have קוקה־קולה too. Kosher for Passover, but still the real thing.

Halfway through hearing everyone's haftorah portions chanted even more haltingly than the week before, the defeated Bar Mitzvah coach declared a break, and we funneled out into the hallway. I bought a sweating, lukewarm Coke, looking away as Zack tried to feed the popped-off bottlecaps back through the coin slot. (The real "hoodlums," as the Junior Congregation rabbi called them, were able to stick their arms up the dispenser at the bottom and pull the bottles loose, like a vet delivering a breached calf.)

At least we were allowed to wear pants to Sunday classes, although girls still could not wear jeans. I was wearing a pair of brick-pink, elastic-waisted pants I'd struggled over in Home Ec, sewing and re-sewing the bunched seams, which were still not straight. I had to wear them somewhere, though, and their discomfort matched perfectly this gray day of sheet rain. I drank the disappointing Coke, so different from the glory I continued to imagine–like every other object in this synagogue, it seemed flatly devoid of mystery. From the licorice taste of the Hadassah sponge cake fingers, to the playground's wonky swings, to the locked Sukkot filled with dead leaves, where was the power? Where was the God who would swoop down to write on the wall, or demand our parents sacrifice us? The Eternal Light's glow in a darkened sanctuary could inspire a little shiver, but that was about it.

A grinding sound came from the Coke machine, and before I could get in trouble for being a witness to Zack's coin-slot destruction, I escaped into the restroom. There, in the yellow light of the stall, I saw the stain on my brick-pink pants and, with a cold, sinking feeling, knew what it was. My first period. The real thing. And I didn't even have a bra yet.

The ladies' room smelled of wet paper towels, and the light was too jaundiced to let me really see. The stain looked more like an inkblot than anything: how miserably perfect that it should happen here, I thought, where I'd spent so many unwilling hours. Now my years of Sunday School would always culminate in this absurd memory.

I had no purse, nor a pair of the dime-holding loafers our Scout leader had told us to wear for just this emergency—nor was there even a machine with a predictably broken coin crank and picture of a calm, poised nurse. So I stalled, prayed for invisibility, and inched back to the classroom, where the fact that no one batted an eye meant the teacher and unofficial minyan of twelve-year-olds had surely guessed my horribly private business.

Through the long ride home with the Goldsteins, I perched on the edge of the vinyl seat, sick from stale cigar fumes and the aftertaste of cola syrup, trying to think of the words I'd need to break this to my mother. The windows steamed up as the gray rain poured on; my arms chafed inside a hot raincoat I knew I could not take off. If I'd never stepped out into that hallway, I suspected, and never bought that sub-standard Coke, and never been aggravated by Zack's antics and the adenoidal droning of my classmates, things could have gone better and this unwelcome initiation might well have held off.

◆

From the golden Hilltop to Olympic Moments to American Idol and even a Bachelor finale, it's clear the masterminds at Coca-Cola want us to associate their product (God forbid it be called a "drink") with the peaks—those utterly uncomplex, photographable moments that chart the highest points on the graph of your life…as if such pure and plottable points even exist. Certainly Coke bubbled through my own Wonder Years, yet from that first high point on the Hilltop, as I practiced my movie-star kiss, the trajectory descended, with each new Coke marking an ever deeper plunge into the murky adolescent abyss.

◆

My third life-jarring romance with Coke was actually Tab—the original, saccharine formula, dark as prune juice, that came in pebbled bottles with cryptic yellow print. This was almost a year before the tired-tasting pink cans appeared, in our state, at least. (Canned Fresca, flavored with equal parts grapefruit and shampoo, had reigned long already as the drink of babysitters.) Decades before Diet Coke, Tab was a forcibly acquired taste—that is, acquired in the way a naive teen might force herself to like

Wild Turkey at a driveway party. The flavor was awful enough to convince American gals that the poison was doing its work, and the carbonation felt harsh enough to be slenderizing all by itself. And if the bottles were chilled almost down to freezing, the taste wasn't so obvious.

That first Tab was handed to me by the unlikeliest of girls: Rachel was counter-culture to the max, far beyond caring about bras, hobbit feet, or the glassy, knowing red of her eyes. And, yet she was the most successfully seductive of all us *nubiles*–the drama teacher's word–as it turned out. In her paisley smock and white painter's pants that showed skin through a frayed square, Rachel tossed me one of the bottles she'd ripped off from our school machine. "Say, 'we're going on a diet,'" she proclaimed, like it was just one more lark–just the way she'd declared that every-one would drop acid April 24 or have a hitchhiking race to the National Mall and back. Rachel was easy to idolize because she was so vividly in-the-moment, as we all aspired to be. *Be here now,* we commanded each other, half-joking, but she was here now, and now, with a vengeance. Rachel was appetite itself, so when she declared a diet, it seemed unlikely, yet a gesture of friendship easier for me to share than a hash joint or a trip to the urban clinic where the girls all got their IUDs.

For Rachel, a diet meant drinking Tab (or mixing rum and Tab on the smoking court), eating chips without the usual roast beef sub, and smoking more pot, which somehow killed her appetite as it jacked up everyone else's. With her cascading kinky hair, she was what I longed to be, despite her blackened feet, upturned nose, and the doughy waist she liked to pinch over the top of her jeans. At home she could get laid and even smoke pot with a bong made from a vacuum cleaner pipe, right up-stairs from her tiny, grandmother-ish mother, who, with her cat-eye glasses, resem-bled a timid Flannery O'Connor. Rachel's father was divorced and a callous creep by reputation, long before such dads were commonplace in the suburbs. She hated to visit but sometimes ran into him at a neighborhood bar, where he'd bum money in exchange for buying her machine cigarettes.

Rachel spoke in a self-conscious slide whistle of a style that simultaneously savored words and made fun of them–everything was pronounced in quotes, and she began most sentences with the word "say," as in "say, 'my car is a junk pit,'" the way a mom might speak for a baby and wave its arm. Rarely did Rachel say anything straight, except once, months later, when I asked her if she'd been seeing Duane, the guy I'd hoped was my boyfriend and she answered simply, "I thought you knew that." I jolted to earth then, but like everything else, this barely seemed to faze her.

Rachel wasn't an earth mother–our hippie high school had several–but she was fearlessly, unbeautifully sexual, in a way you'd never see on TV. She'd sit in the hall-way with her best friend on her lap, finger-combing the girl's flame-red hair where it spilled from her bandana, blabbering about blowjobs and payback; she wore out-of-character wire frame glasses and a serious expression only when she drove herself.

In any case, hedonist Rachel was the last girl in the world you'd expect to propose a diet, but she did as we sat out on the straw-yellow grass, toasting the notion with the bottles of warm Tab she'd stolen for both us. In hindsight, that might have been when she'd started screwing Duane, whom I'd adored since February, but whatever the inspiration, we basked on the school's ragged spring lawn, breathing in the first hints of humidity and honeysuckle, and throwing back medicinal shots of Tab together.

That was the first step, and from there our paths split. Rachel worked off two pounds by having sex, she said, letting me think she meant with her best friend's brother. Her "lust life" sounded easy, while my heart thumped sickly every time the phone would ring, and I filled the time between rare Friday evening summons from Duane with weighing and measuring foods according to my father's neglected diet-and-calorie guide. Worried by my determination, my mother banned the few diet foods I could scrounge up, just as she had the old longed-for junk food—first my hidden stash of Ayds was forbidden, then the bread made with wood shavings, and finally fake diabetic chocolate ice cream the color of Quick Tan. But I lost 46 pounds in the next six months, through counting calories down to fractions, marching miles around the block in sizzling heat, and straining to learn ballet with elementary school girls.

I got dumped by Duane and told the truth by Rachel after she'd abandoned the diet in favorite of actual cocaine, the real real thing, which for her did the weight-loss trick with much less trouble and also helped her waitress double-shifts in a seafood house where the smell of deep-fried shrimp infused her hair and spilled sweet tea granulated her skin. With my palms yellowed by carrots, I turned full-on anorexic with grief. If Duane couldn't find me beautiful like this, well, at least he'd have to pay attention, I wrongly thought, and finally get "worried," like the rest of our crew. Instead, he moved away to Alabama.

Tab became my lifeblood but was banned from my house, and outside, people frowned when I drank it after I sank below 100 pounds. Despite the taste, I drank my Tab warm when I could get it, as the slightest chill would freeze me. Every afternoon I crashed and huddled on the sunlit couch in a wrap-around patchwork sweater, clutching my clavicles, scribbling Joni Mitchell imitations, and conjuring the memory of Duane's every tobacco-flavored kiss and weary monosyllable. I turned into such a skeleton that even my bone-loving ballet teacher chided me; Rachel became a star waitress who worked so much I could never see her, and from a party, in the middle of an Allman Brothers riff, Duane took off for the Heart of Dixie without so much as a glance back at me.

I remember few Tab commercials—just a bottle sucking its sides into an hourglass silhouette—but it didn't take perfect harmonies for Tab to sell itself to girls like me. Alone at 89 pounds, caged in my perfect, graspable skeleton of grief, a year from U-turning to gain back every pound, what stuck in my head was not a jingle or slogan, but the spring fever pact we'd made that afternoon in the grass: my too-real passion bubbling up through pebbled glass, Rachel's lilting laugh, and the first enchanted, syrupy dose of that most artificial of all drinks.

Now, as a mid-life adult free to let my cravings rage as high as 300 or more liters of Diet Coke a year, it's finally becoming the pause that depresses—the choice between enduring another morning headache without it or succumbing and setting off another mini-bout of guilt. My friends and I still scarf down the diet drinks, stocking up during Dollar Days at Walgreens, but Diet Coke too has joined the ranks of virtuous foods gone bad: the dentist says it has acid-washed my tooth enamel and must be quit; the doctor scolds that there's as much caffeine in a Diet Coke as a cup of coffee, which doesn't feel any more true than it did the first time he said it; and the women's magazines, having earned maximum mileage from assuring that diet drinks don't cause cancer, now feature colorful call-outs of the newest research showing that artificial sweeteners overtax the kidneys and lead to early failure and, perhaps worse, somehow counteract efforts at weight loss by convincing your brain to consume the calories that ought to match the drinks' sweetness level. At best, according to the insufferable Dr. Oz, diet soda makes the body crave sweet things all the more. Perhaps this explains the credo every dieter knows—that the perfect pairing with brownies is always Diet Coke.

Water is the best drink! is every professional's bubbly advice. And no, sadly, they don't even mean water made palatable by so much as a tincture of Crystal Lite. So some days I strain to get my bubble fix from plain seltzer; while other, weaker days I'm left pondering the mystery of why a 32-ounce bottle of soda can cost 99 cents on special, but the 16-ounce bottles at the grocery checkout never dip below $1.49. Of course the Coke moguls have that one all figured out, knowing that while we might chug from a 2-liter soda bottle at home, no grocery-bearing woman desperate for her fix wants to be seen doing that in her car, or in front of her kids, or having to use her clenched knees as a cupholder. Although it can be done, let me be the first to tell you.

...Apple trees, honey bees, harmony, company, and the snow-white polar bears of love...

Even today, is it possible to watch a Coke commercial and not be filled with longing—for memories that don't even exist? Real or aspartame, with the Real Thing, is there even any difference?

An Offering
Ray McManus

A blurred church.
A boy in the middle
of a half-finished foyer.
Plaster falls in slow
motion like ash
over rebar crosses.
Boot. Wall. Fist.
Boot. Wall. Fist.
Boot. Wall. Fist.
Dust falls over
the open door,
a silhouette.
The sound of feet
dragging in the dark.

Damage
Jody Hobbs Hesler

David Weld's cell phone vibrated on the desktop in the middle of his meeting, his old home number showing on the screen. David had volunteered to stay late with his boss to help crunch numbers for their quarterly meeting next morning. Back when he and Trudy were still married, he had volunteered for overtime, angling for promotions and raises for the extra money for college funds, the next vacation, Trudy's latest new car. Now he needed the money for child support and his new mortgage, and the overtime delayed his return to his empty house.

The phone rang again, and David considered ignoring it, which was his norm before the separation. Trudy would snap at him afterward, "Do you think I'm calling to chat?" as if that were the most disgusting of possibilities. It was true that she didn't call often, and usually her calls meant something was wrong. Once, work had kept him from taking one of Trudy's calls when it turned out their older daughter, Ginnie had broken her leg jumping hurdles at a track meet. Work had also kept him from remembering the meet. It was always worse to ignore the phone, so, finally, David risked the impatient glance of his boss and answered.

This time, it wasn't Trudy. "There's smoke, Dad. Smoke's coming in." It was his younger daughter, Layna, just turned thirteen.

"Jesus, Layna. Where's your mom? Your sister?" But all he could hear on the other end was Layna, breathing fast, and the smoke alarm's syncopated screech. The office and his boss's face blurred into the background. "You need to get out of the house."

"It's coming in under the front door. Dad! Shit! I don't know what to do."

"I do," David said. "Go see if there's any smoke at the back door." He stayed on the line while she walked through the house. There was no smoke there. "Now go outside, Layna. To our safe spot. Remember, from fire safety?" Back when she had been in elementary school, a paper had come home during fire prevention week that outlined steps for fire safety. One step was drawing up a plan and having family fire drills. That had sounded extreme to David at the time, but misfiring smoke detectors had given them plenty of chances to practice anyway. Their safe spot was the stop sign in the far corner of their front yard. "Now let's hang up and we'll both call 9-1-1. Okay?" The phone went dead. David's hands shook.

He dialed 9-1-1 and fed the operator what little information he had. His boss's eyebrows tented in alarm. When David stood up, he could hardly feel his legs. He said, "I have to –" and his boss nodded and waved him on. Just like Trudy used to tell him, "You don't get fired for having a family, David. Jesus."

David scraped his files from the edge of his boss's desk into his briefcase and rushed toward his car. He tried calling Layna again, but the line went straight to voice mail. Same thing happened when he tried Ginnie. Were his daughters safe? Was the house they had lived in since they were born burning down?

It was past rush hour, but traffic was unnerving. Slow driver here, too-long red light there. The world seemed full of idiots.

Half the time, he was the idiot. It was a shock Layna would think to call him in an emergency. He was determined not to let her down the way he usually did, like when he'd been in another meeting and had forgotten to pick her up from an after-school club, back before the separation. The assistant principal had finally driven her home, then waited on the front steps until someone got there. Of course Trudy had arrived first; she always got home from work on time. Where was she tonight?

Fire engines crowded the street in front of David's old house. Flashing red lights sliced in and out of the dark. Dissipating smoke around the front porch shimmered in lifting red clouds into the dark. In the yard, firemen shouted back and forth and unrolled or re-rolled lengths of hose.

The sirens shrieked to a stop just before David got out of his car, but the lights kept strobing. In one flash, the neon strips on a fireman's uniform caught the glare of David's headlights, and he finally saw Layna, right beside the fireman, crouching at the base of the stop sign. The way Layna huddled there made her look half her thirteen years at best.

David ran and stooped beside her, hugging her and saying her name and, "Thank God," over and over. A thick wool blanket draped her shoulders, something the fireman must have given her.

The fireman stood and ceded the post beside Layna. "Here's what we know," he said. "No one else was home. Your daughter here's fine, but pretty shook up. Looks like somebody stuck a smoke bomb between the storm door and the front door. It made a mess, but nothing caught fire. We're looking at damages, checking everything out, making sure that's all there was. Should be okay for y'all to head back inside any minute."

David's other daughter Ginnie jogged up as the fireman went to rejoin his crew in the yard. "Dad?" She seemed as surprised to see him as she was to see the fire engines. She bent over her little sister. "Are you okay?"

Next on the scene came Trudy, squealing her car to a halt and bolting out of it, panning the dark yard and calling, "Girls? Dear God. Girls?"

David shouted, "Over here!" and Trudy's hand dropped across her heart, the first time she had been relieved to see him in longer than David could remember. Now, with Layna leaning into his arms, Ginnie standing behind him – one hand on his shoulder, one hand trailing softly through Layna's hair – and Trudy completing their circle, they'd seem like the perfect tableau of a family to anyone passing by.

"The fireman said it was a smoke bomb," David explained.

Another fireman shouted from the porch, "Y'all can go ahead inside now. House is clear." Near the house, another fireman waved them toward the back door, away from the huddle of firemen inspecting the front door. A smoky funk hung in the air. David and his family climbed the deck stairs to the back door.

Inside, the funky smell was fainter. Smudges on the white rugs showed where firemen's boots had trod, helter-skelter, as they checked the house for other dangers.

In the living room, Trudy settled into the overstuffed chair, doing her best to cradle Layna in her lap. Since the separation, Trudy had controlled the girls' pick-ups and drop-offs so that David hardly made it past the foyer anymore. The living room felt unfamiliar now, with a new sofa, new TV, and even the old end tables in new places. When everyone began talking about what happened, David started to feel as if he hadn't been a part of any of it.

"I was at the grocery store," Trudy said. "I'd left my cell phone charging."

Ginnie said, "I was hanging out at Lisa's," her friend down the block, "and I took off running when I saw fire trucks headed for our end of the street. Still, I didn't think it was our house."

Layna said, "I called Mom and I could hear her phone ringing. Right over there." She pointed toward the island separating the living room and kitchen. David looked, but couldn't see a phone among all the books and after-school snack dishes yet to be cleared. But now he knew why he'd been called in for the emergency.

"A smoke bomb?" Trudy said, as if the news of it had just hit her. "Was this supposed to be some kind of joke?" Trudy's eyes met David's. Layna and Ginnie looked to him, too. He wanted to give them answers, assurances, but he didn't know what to say.

Instead, he said, "Are there groceries in the car?" He knew what to do with groceries.

Outside in the cold, David threaded his way through firemen and fire engines to where Trudy's car stood, door yawning open, keys still hanging from the ignition. As he made his way back to the house, bags braced to his chest and two more clutched in his hands, one of the firemen caught his attention. "Looks like all cosmetic damage. You're looking at a couple new doors, maybe some wood for the threshold. Nothing structural, though."

Inside, bright lights from idling fire trucks pulsed red down the white hallway. Layna still clung to her mother. Ginnie sat across from them on the sofa, talking on her phone about the prank. "Some asshole, getting his jollies scaring my little sister." David could see Layna shivering against her mother, fear still gripping her. It was weird how a feeling could outlast its cause so long.

Unloading groceries in the kitchen helped David hide it, but he was shaking, too. It had only been a smoke bomb, but when Layna called, all he had known was that something bad had happened, and he hadn't been here to stop it.

He kept busy in the kitchen as long as he could. When a knock came at the door, David told Trudy he'd get it. It was Jerry, a police officer David knew because he lived a few streets down. He was on duty now. They stood in the foyer to talk. David wondered if he had heard about the divorce.

"Some neighbor kid with a Bear Cat scanner heard Dispatch call in the response for Layna. He saw some boys running off down the street, recognized them," Jerry said. He told David which boys they were. "You know them, David. Good families, decent kids."

The boys had lived in the neighborhood for ages, played ball at the end of this street sometimes, just started getting acne and forgetting how to talk around Ginnie. They were a little rowdy, but they knew how to flash their Huck Finn smiles and say, "Yes, sir," in time to stay this side of trouble.

"What they wanted," Jerry said, "was for Ginnie to be home and get spooked just enough to run outside so they could all get a look at her." Laugh lines crinkled Jerry's eyes. "You believe that? Bunch of goofballs."

David believed it. At sixteen, Ginnie looked twenty: full body, pouty lips, eyes full of invitation. The smoke bomb stunt, if it had gone as planned, would have given those boys the chance to see her without having to think up something cool to say. But the thought of three lanky, zit-pocked teenagers so eager to look at his daughter made David's stomach roll. So did knowing that if he had thought of it way back when, he might have tried the same trick on Ruth Bentley on Jackson Street, too pretty to talk to him when he was just fifteen.

But it had been Layna, home alone, who saw smoke seeping in under the front door. Had those boys had the nerve to feel disappointed when Layna had been the one to come outside? Had they watched her struggle, terrified, toward the stop sign before they loped away, unscathed?

"So, whaddaya think, Dave, maybe you get them boys down here to help fix up the damage? Pay for it and do the work, too? They keep their records clean and you get them to put everything back the way it was?"

David didn't answer. Why should he let anyone off easy? Besides, he knew better than most that you can never put things back the way they were.

Jerry noticed David's hesitation, took a step back as if to make physical space for a different opinion. "Hey, we can send up charges to the juvenile court. But I'll tell you, that big kid, Tommy? I come to the door, he's got tears in his eyes. Keeps asking if everybody's okay. He never guessed anybody'd call 9-1-1, and when he saw those fire engines, he figured the whole house was burning down. I'll be honest, man, I let him ask about four times before I told him everybody was okay. The rest of those boys hung behind Tommy, scared shitless. They know they screwed up, if you're worried about that."

"Yeah, I'm worried about that," David said.

Trudy must have managed to slide Layna into the chair by herself for a minute. She joined David and Jerry in the foyer. Jerry brought Trudy up to date about the boys and the offer for them to fix things up instead of going to court. Trudy looked to David, seemed to defer the decision to him, even though she didn't do that anymore. A few weeks ago, he had offered to replace the spotlight over the garage when he'd noticed it was out, and she'd squawked about how it was her house now and he had to quit acting like it wasn't. It was fixed now, too, beaming a steady yellow swath of light that the fire engines' red lights kept criss-crossing.

It felt good for Trudy to let him help, so he thought about what was at stake. The incident had turned out to be horrifying, but the boys hadn't figured on that part. In the end, it was just a smoke bomb, a typical teen boy prank. It wasn't supposed to cause a fire, and it hadn't. Some things, when they were meant to be small, or nothing at all, deserved second chances. So David said, "Okay. The boys can help fix it."

Trudy nodded, accepting his decision. "You'll have to work with them, though. I don't want to look at them."

About the same time Jerry left, the fire engines' lights flashed off, leaving a moment's reddish glow in the darkness. Warning beeps sounded, and the trucks finally backed out and away from the house.

Back in the living room, Layna curled against her mother again. It was seven thirty. David said, "I'm calling out for pizza. It's late and we're all hungry." The way Trudy looked at him, he could tell she wouldn't have deferred the decision about pizza to him. He had outstayed the feeling that this house ever could have been his.

A few minutes later at the door, David noticed the pizza guy checking out the smoke damage. David joked, "Yeah, it's been a hot night in here." The pizza guy looked at him funny, as if even he could tell David didn't live here anymore.

The pizza left a sheen on David's hands and made his stomach feel like a fist. When it was gone, he knew it was time for him to leave. But the pizza smell had subsided, and David noticed that the sulphur after-stench of the smoke bomb, which hadn't been much at first, now reeked throughout the house. And Layna already looked as if she'd been up three days straight. David couldn't imagine her falling asleep tonight in a house that stunk of smoke bomb.

David dragged a hand across his face, wondered if he looked as tired as Layna. "Why don't you all come back to my house tonight?" he suggested. "That way, even though it's cold, you could leave some windows open here, air the place out."

Trudy considered his offer. But David knew, even if she wanted to come, she'd talk herself out of it. She was letting him help today because it was best for the girls, not because she missed him. She didn't wake up mornings, twisted in the sheets, aching for the feel of his flesh, the smell of his hair.

"I'll be fine here, David," Trudy said, and he knew she would be. "But the girls can go with you if they want."

Ginnie was sitting beside her mother on the sofa, texting one of her friends. She became aware of the conversation around her and tucked the phone into her pocket. "Will you be all right here by yourself?" she asked Trudy.

"Sure, honey." Trudy leaned over and kissed Ginnie's forehead.

At some point, David had stopped doing that, kissing their foreheads, their cheeks. He thought if he did it now, it would be weird. But they used to climb into his lap, wet from bathtimes, smelling like flowers. He would burrow his nose into their wet hair, tickle their sides, smother their little bellies in raspberries.

David's house smelled the same way it always did: sawdust, a faint odor of new paint. The girls unloaded into the house the way they always did, too, like visitors, carrying duffel bags and leaving their shoes neatly at the door. His leather sofas squeaked and exhaled when they sank into the cushions, balancing their school books in their laps to finish the homework they had nearly forgotten. Layna hooked her ipod into David's music system, and the sounds of her favorite pop bands felt unfamiliar in the air. No wonder they spent all their time with him texting friends and playing video games on their little handheld gadgets. There was nothing about this house that felt like it was theirs.

But it didn't smell like a smoke bomb. So when bedtime came around, they got ready as if it were a normal night. David leaned into each of their bedroom doors to say good night. The girls peeked out at him from underneath bedspreads they'd had when they were younger. He had thought the old spreads would make their rooms feel homey, but now he could see now that they just made the rooms seem out of whack.

David stayed up late, going through the papers he had stuffed into his briefcase hours before. So he was awake to hear the light shuffle of Layna's footsteps around midnight. He peered into the hall and watched Layna walk slowly to the top of the steps, crane forward, as if she were listening for something, then feel her hand along the wall there.

"Layna?" he whispered, trying not to startle her, but she gasped and whipped her neck around toward him anyway. That fire safety awareness program in elementary school had trained the children how to tell if your house was on fire. You went to the top the stairs and listened, then tested the walls for heat. "Honey, what're you doing?"

"Nothing," she said, but she didn't move her hand from the wall.

"Sweetheart, there's no fire." He was beside her now, pulling her close. "There's no fire." He left his papers strewn across his bed and pulled a sleeping bag onto the floor of Layna's room.

Twice that night, she woke up screaming. David reached his hand up to the side of the bed, and Layna kept clutching onto it, long after they both fell asleep again.

The day the boys came to do their repairs, they brought some tools and money for supplies David had bought. David showed them the new storm door, the new

Illustration by Stephen Smith

strip of wood for the threshold, the new front door, and all the woodwork that needed sanding, priming, and re-painting. He explained what needed to be done. They kept serious looks on their faces and said, "Yes, sir, Mr. Weld."

It was early April now, sunny and hot. The boys did all the work without complaining. David was surprised. Near the end of the job, he told them, "You know, you're doing really good work."

"Thanks, Mr. Weld." The boys grinned. "We didn't mean any trouble."

They were trying to make good with him now, maybe practicing for when they hoped to come pick Ginnie up for a date sometime. They probably didn't know David wouldn't be the parent to answer this door they were re-building together.

Every now and then, David saw Ginnie's curtain flapping upstairs. He had told her to find something else to do, but she had overheard how these boys had pulled this prank just to catch sight of her. Now she was trying to catch sight of them, their muscles gleaming with sweat, working to make things right.

"Layna has nightmares," David said, because she did, one every night since the smoke bomb. One at a time, he looked each of the boys in the eyes. "Every night she wakes up screaming. She thinks the house is burning down." The boys turned away from him, all their grins gone, and they sought out spots along the sidewalk where they could look without meeting David's eyes. "Every night."

The sun was bearing down on their backs. David could feel it burning the flesh of his neck. But he thought it should have been hotter, or the work should have been harder. It had only been a little sanding and hammering and painting. The boys were laughing.

Too soon, the work was finished. The boys began packing up their things. They lined up, right by the stop sign, the family's safe spot. One of them tried to tell David good-bye or thank you, and David tried to think of something to say. No matter what any of them had meant to happen, everywhere boys were trying to look at girls, trying to figure out how to please them; girls were wanting them to. Something always went wrong. In this family, it had gone wrong way before these boys even showed up.

Ginnie's bedroom window whooshed open above their heads. "Hey, assholes! Next time just knock on the damn door!" Then she slammed the window shut. Her laughter rang out through the glass. Even Layna was giggling.

The Huck Finn smiles spread across their faces. All three boys swaggered off down the street.

Last Course
Claire McQuerry

I grew up despite my best efforts.
Apricots rained on the trampoline
and rotted in the long grasses. The apricot's
seam is darker than its surface and asks
to be swung apart like saloon doors. Games
we played involved this splitting, the doll's
vessel where the pit grew: the halves of fruit
would fill each morning if left beside
the tree. In this, an apricot resembles

the holy well at Cernay: though the masonry's
in ruins, the well retains its lip of moss.
(In ruins, though, like any war-struck
marvel, suggesting an imaginary whole.)
The queen drank and *her womb*, some
histories say, *unlocked*. The king despised her
politicking, but eleven live births is
another story. Knocked up: this miracle
won the abbot great favor (it was his

well) and purses weighted with gold. Well-made
purses, like dresses, get linings. The lining,
mother said, should be sumptuous: velvet,
perhaps, or satin; the hand inside should
feel caressed. We children would fill
them with coins or anything that rang
together when we played, lipstick,
mirrors, mimicking the seductively
grown-up. Like many others, this game

was nameless. Mother named me
as soon as she knew she was
pregnant. The name means *clear* or
light, a word like a window and airy,
belonging as it does to the saint, who

trailed the nothing on which she feasted
in tiers of wind and straw. Clare
is lauded for refusal as much as for love
of the poor. I don't even refuse

dessert. Once, many dinners ended
with fruit. Mother simmered apricots
with sugar and clove and ladled
the compote over ice-cream. The man to her
left put his ear to mother's mouth. Conversation
at the long table was kaleidoscopic—
I fought to hear any one voice. "Can't you
sense the chemistry?" mother turned
to me. She meant the man. She sparkled

with diamonds, though she wore
no diamonds. My father, at the other
end of the table, where the vase of poppies
had been moved aside, was shipwrecked.
I understood then that love
loves nothing so much as the nothing
it leaves on its plate.

Stratigraphy
Claire McQuerry

Take what's unearthed—copper, bone
needles, silver coins—as evidence of continuous
human presence. Such odd detritus
and handiwork: this bronze
ear pick etched with fine cross-hatch or that
female figurine of painted clay, "meaning
unknown," striped and small enough
to wrap in your hand. They look as if
laid aside yesterday, signs of commerce
or devotion. Bronze handle of a mirror,
pottery shards which offer a partial
story: the hands of Paris presenting the apple
to Aphrodite. Someone stands beside
the goddess, but only her feet
and robes remain. How much is
unknowable and lost to us,
how much surmised. Dig until you find
a comb, further down an amphora's handle,
a seal. Here's sign of fire, here
erosion, here time
piling its jewels and ash, spreading
its quilts over the dead.

Settlement
Claire McQuerry

The game's called Settlers and involves
a balance of strategy and chance,
which I navigate by counting heavily
on luck, trusting my erratic tactics
to pull me through. He ponders, and always,
when it looks as though he'll lose,
he rallies at the last. This is the strategy
I lack; I can only will him to draw
an unfavorable hand: all bricks, no wheat,
or another ore card, when he needs
just one more sheep to cash in
a settlement at the end
of his carefully positioned road.

* * * *

When I say I'll move to a new place
I give him a litany of reasons
that satisfy, but I know my own:
no strategy at all. The flight
instinct that keeps me
always moving. When I can't
change cities, I change houses. I get
in my car with a full tank of gas
and feel the rising relief. Long-
distance is the only relationship
I do; a loophole in itself.

* * * *

One night, when I couldn't sleep
I rose and wrote
a letter I wouldn't send: *You
have made a home in your
city; I don't know*

whether I could make
a home with you.

* * * *

What does it mean to settle?
The glitter in a shook
snow globe; dust on the lip
of a bookshelf I never wipe; or
in the end, she settled for him
because he was kind enough
and she felt time shuttling past.

* * * *

He has surrounded himself
with friends in this city. He can name
neighborhoods, good people who live
in this or that house we pass, parks
he used to cross as a younger man.
He bakes bread for neighbors, and they
bring him apples, cucumber, eggs.
They wave from the front porch.
Where's the back door, I wonder, the trick
card he keeps up his sleeve?

* * * *

I draw a thief card and move
into the ore mines beside his settlement.
For four rounds we play
this way, my thief, skimming
ore off the top of every roll,
thwarting his strategy.
In the morning I will catch a plane.
We will both decide
I'm not the object he's after.

Kerry
Ian Hoppe

"I mean, what am I, a fuckin' sailor?" he slurred as he did the one-eye drunk-squint out of the windshield of his brand new, base model F-150.

We were barreling down Highway 90 along the Mississippi coast, weaving in and out of traffic in the morning sun. My head was bobbing with each movement of the steering wheel, turning on occasion to stare droopy-faced at the angry morning commuters we were passing.

We had spent the last three hours at The Miss-A-Bama, an aptly named bar in a prefab metal building on Highway 90 near the Mississippi-Alabama line. I was only eighteen, but the middle-aged, rough-cut bartender said I looked like Russell Crowe, so she let me drink and even bought me a couple of Miller High-Life and several shots of Jack Daniel's. We left because Kerry got mad and kicked the bathroom stall door off of its hinges. I don't remember why.

We were electricians working the night shift at Signal International Shipyard in Pascagoula, Mississippi. We had been working 7 days a week, 12-14 hours per day for the last two months and would be for the foreseeable future.

When Hurricane Katrina was crawling across the gulf, the crews on floating drill rigs were evacuated. The rigs themselves ended up getting pushed into the Louisiana Delta and flipped onto their side, where they lay for months afterwards. Crews were slowly collecting them, turning them upright, and towing them into the gulf shipyards for clean-up and renovation. The East Yard, where we were working, had four square bays in which these rigs were parked. The whole place was surrounded by a ten foot chain-link fence topped with three strands of rusty barbed wire. The actual bays were a small part of the overall yard, most of which was warehouses, administrative and communication offices, fabrication buildings, and worn-out trailers that housed the large and seemingly incarcerated population of Indian welders and painters; fodder for another story.

The process of returning these rigs to working order was grueling. Because of the huge number of these rigs that were damaged, the schedule for a complete rebuild was roughly a month. That included demolition of all existing electrical and mechanical components, reinstallation, inspections, and a fresh coat of paint on everything. This kind of timeline meant everyone was constantly working on top of each other, the stress level was high, and the heat was especially oppressive.

What Kerry was angry about was the announcement at the end of the previous shift that if the rig we were working on wasn't finished by the scheduled date, it would be towed to its next drilling location off the coast of Brazil with a select crew aboard to finish the job en route. And, given the drill-pit fire that had occurred the previous night, setting us back several hours, we were not going to be done on time.

I was excited about the prospect; Kerry was not. Though I never saw any physical evidence of it, I got the feeling that he had a methamphetamine problem, mostly because of his fast tic, periodic outbursts, and how it seemed like all of the veins on his upper body were trying to force their way through his skin. Even on his fingers, a skinny bump traveled all the way from the back of his hand to the cuticle, like some kind of grotesque anatomy figure.

The first to board any arriving rig was a group of burly animal control agents. Having been strewn across the delta like a toddler's toys for several months, the rigs made a great home for various, terrifying genera of snakes and the occasional pissed-off alligator in the mud room. Next, there was an overall inspection of the state of the rig and a comprehensive plan and timeline was developed within a few hours. By the time our boots hit the metal grating of the main deck, every night was planned, down to the very last cable.

I started on the cable pulling team. We fumbled around in the heavy darkness with headlamps and ratcheting cable cutters and removed every piece of the 1970s, asbestos marine cable from the ship. Some of the cable was as big around as my thigh. We had to cut it with a sawzall and carry it out piece by piece on our shoulders, dumping it into huge buckets that were lifted from the rig by the tower crane that loomed over the ship. After all of it had been removed, we spent several days working with the welders, reforming the miles of cable tray that scaled every wall and covered every ceiling, bit by bit. None of the welders spoke English, but it didn't matter since the noise of the huge banks of welders and generators reverberated through the metal hull of the structure at such a pitch that the drive back to the hotel at the end of the shift in my rusty '73 Chevrolet with no muffler seemed like overbearing silence.

The communication was almost entirely non-verbal, a series of signs that was developed and molded by the crew. The high-pitched whooping, which could be heard through the foam earplugs we were required to wear, was used to signal different things, depending on the activity. I was surprised at how efficient and fast paced this communicative system was considering the variance of languages, dialects, and cultures we had on each team.

The huge spools of cable were lifted onto the rig by way of the tower crane and placed near a porthole, or stairway, or cable chase where they were balanced on a thick piece of rigid pipe. Four of the bigger guys would then lift in onto a set of rolling jacks that would allow the spool to turn. We would line up smallest to largest and climb head first into the hole in 10-15 foot increments, the first guy dragging the end of the cable along its specific route, the rest of us spreading out equally on the tray and jerking the cable along. The foreman stayed at the spool controlling its rate of turn. When a bulkhead was reached, the lead would let out a loud "whoop!" which would travel successively back to the foreman who would stop feeding the cable. The lead would climb down from the rack and find his way to the other side, the second puller would move against the bulkhead, and everyone would spread themselves equally between them, collecting around corners and rises.

When the lead had found the other side of the bulkhead and made his way onto the rack, the second would send a "whoop!" up the line and the pulling would continue, slowly feeding and routing the cable until it reached its destination and we would hear a longer "whoop!", settle our portion of cable neatly into the rack, climb down from our perch, and meet with the foreman to plan the next pull. We did this hundreds of times for hundreds of cables of different sizes and weights, and we were good at it. The ends of the cable were coiled, labeled with numbers associated with the design prints and left hanging. They would be terminated by the day crew the following morning.

My first night on the yard, I was placed on a different rig, which was in the final week of the renovation. The rig was much larger and the crews were experienced and fast. I'll never forget walking into the main engine room, where four Caterpillar diesel engines the size of school busses stood in a row running at full capacity. The room was incredibly hot from a combination of the activity, generators, and beating Mississippi sun that had just set. Welder's blinding light flashed off of the metal walls and pipe fitters screamed at one another and banged on huge metal exhaust pipes. And the electricians scampered, in huge synchronized groups, on the canopy of crisscrossed racks overhead whooping loudly and raining huge, labored drops of blackened sweat on the generators and workers below, causing a steam to fill the room from top to bottom that smelled like sweat, smoldering metal and diesel fuel.

It was beautiful. It was like a fucking jungle.

When we got off work, we looked like coal miners, black from head to foot except for the strip across our eyes where the requisite safety glasses were strapped. Our clothes were completely drenched with sweat. I got in the habit of taking multiple shirts with me on my shift, just to retain some sense of comfort. After a couple of welders suffered heat strokes, we were required to take five minute breaks once every two hours and drink a quart of water under the supervision of our foreman.

When the shift was over, we would stack our tools in the gang-box and line up at the buck-hoist, which would take us down to the surface of the yard where we clocked out and stumbled through the gate to our vehicles.

One particular night, we got off at 6:30am, passing the day crew we had seen 12 hours before at the turnstiles on our way to the huge dirt parking lot filled with aging Chevrolet short-beds and beat up Toyota Corollas that were plastered with local union numbers and Bush '00 stickers.

Up until this point, I had lived a fairly quiet and solitary life in an extended stay motel down the road. I was rooming with a huge, racist bald man who worked day shift in the same yard, so I never saw him. At a lull in the action, Kerry had somehow convinced me that we should drink some beers after work, his treat. So we hit the grocery store deli for breakfast and grabbed a 12-pack of Bud Light on the way out the door.

At that age I was not especially practiced in inebriated self-control. And this is how it happened that I was convinced to go with Kerry to his hometown of Calhoun City, Mississippi on a whim.

Calhoun City is just east of Grenada, Mississippi, west of Okalona, and north of Eupora. It is literally in the middle of nowhere, the backwoods, if you will. In fact, Calhoun City may be behind the backwoods, or at least partially obscured by the backwoods.

It was about a five hour drive from Pascagoula. Within that time, I had mostly sobered up and come to terms with my horrible decision. I couldn't show I was terrified because I had been talking big-shit with Kerry all day and he thought I was a badass, which either says something about my persuasiveness or his intellect.

Either way, we stopped at his brother's house somewhere south of Calhoun City so he could come with us. This was a complete surprise to his brother, who seemed taken aback by Kerry's sudden arrival, almost like he hadn't called at all. The guy had a family, a dirty family, but a seemingly happy one, in their tiny trailer sitting several hundred feet from a fairly major highway. There were a couple of kids piddling around in the front yard in various states of undress. When we pulled up, he quickly shut his wife inside and herded the kids to the door. We both got out of the truck and walked towards him, but he and Kerry stepped over to the side to have a personal conversation immediately, leaving me to the side, tamping dirt with my steel-toed boot.

He went inside and grabbed a small bag and we all got back in the truck, Kerry riding in the middle.

I never learned his name, even though we spent a lot of time together in the next 24 hours. This was mainly because of the colossal wad of chewing tobacco that was always tucked away in his cheek. He used nearly an entire can with each dip and packed it with sickening force into his mouth, with the practiced air of a veteran user. At the time he was using his right cheek, but I could see that he used to use his left from the stretch marks on it. Between the omnipresent Copenhagen and the heavy country drawl, we ended up communicating with signs and social cues, much like I did with the foreign workers in the shipyard, when we spoke at all.

Since I couldn't understand him anyway, and because I was nursing a hangover and incredibly sleepy, I ignored their conversation for the rest of the ride to Calhoun City. We rolled into the outskirts of town and started stopping at different houses, trailers, and places of business talking to people. After the first couple of stops it became evident that it had been many years, maybe a decade, since Kerry had been home. And there were two polar reactions to the site of his squinty, scarred face, "Hey, Kerry came home!" or, "Oh shit, Kerry is home." By the time we made it to the fourth or fifth place, the news was ahead of us and the people were expecting him.

The final stop was his mother's house. She too, knew we were coming and was waiting in a chair outside the house when we arrived. I suddenly knew my place. I was the awkward, youngish friend of a prodigal son.

"Who are you?" they would ask.

"I'm the guy that got drunk with Kerry this morning. Nice to meet you." I would answer jovially.

His mother greeted us with caution. Slightly hugging Kerry and looking me up and down suspiciously. "I don't want to be here anymore than you want me here." I tried to tell her with my eyes. They sat on the couch and talked like a family while I passed out in a green recliner for several hours. Maybe I would wake up in the morning, get back to Pascagoula and beg forgiveness from the superintendent. Maybe all this was just a trip home to see Mama. Not so lucky.

Kerry shook me at around ten that night and motioned for me to get up. I could tell he had never quit drinking. We ate some from-frozen chicken fingers over the kitchen sink in the dark and went outside where his brother was waiting in the truck. We drove around for a bit making more stops and surprising more people, eventually getting to a bar called The Dry Dock which has a Confederate flag painted on its dance floor and was packed full of people in their Calhoun City finest, dancing and singing along with the country band on stage. They pulled some kind of strings with the bouncers and got me in. Kerry put a High Life in my hand and I made my way toward the stage.

I was about halfway done with the beer and had just started a conversation with a cute little southern belle who thought I was 21 and seemed fascinated by the story I'm telling you now, when I heard Kerry yell something and turned around to watch him shatter a glass ashtray on another fellow's cheekbone.

Kerry's brother was immediately in the fray, tobacco juice squirting from his mouth like some agitated sprinkler repeatedly punching a seemingly random bystander. I figured that the best way to help would be getting people away from Kerry, so I jumped in and started pushing malicious looking people away from him, which only escalated the situation. When the bouncers finally jumped in, they pushed us out of the front door and the other group of miscreants out the back.

We convened at his truck. The brother was already in the driver's seat staring forward. I got the feeling that he knew this was coming and I was beginning to understand why Kerry hadn't been home for years. Kerry poured himself into the center passenger seat and began pummeling the dashboard screaming nonsensically and sobbing heavily. The blood from his knuckles sprayed onto the windshield, where it would remain, congealed brown, for the duration of our relationship.

He eventually composed himself, to a degree, and exited the truck to retrieve a beer from the cooler in the back. I got one for myself and his brother as Kerry announced that we should "...go find that motherfucker." Apparently, an ashtray to the face was not enough to avenge the horrible wrong that this fellow had inflicted upon him.

It turns out that the guy was the current husband of Kerry's high school sweetheart and had said something demeaning about or to him in the short time we were in the bar. Like a dutiful chauffer, his brother started the car and drove out of the parking lot. Kerry gave him some kind of coordinates that he seemed to understand and we sped down the road in the pitched darkness.

Eventually, we arrived at what Kerry thought was our target's house. I got out of the passenger side and Kerry climbed out after me and slung what was left of his beer into the woods next to the road. He was teetering significantly on the sloped side of the road, but he got his footing after a moment. He told us to keep driving so that no one would know he was there if they returned and to come back in a few minutes.

We didn't speak as he drove down the road and parked in a vacant lot, sipping our beers and looking out into the blackness. Passing the house a few minutes later, we didn't see Kerry or any additional cars. We assumed that he was lying in wait and went the other direction, this time parking on the side of the road and killing the headlights. I'm sure he was wondering just what the hell I was doing there as we turned around and headed back, waiting even longer this time. When we came upon the house again from the opposite direction, he noticed that Kerry had in fact passed out in the ditch on the side of the road where we had left him.

His brother got out of the truck and pulled him up, walking him to the truck and laying him in the seat on top of me. He was still whispering in a calloused voice about all of the horrible things he would do his adversary. When we got back to his mother's house, I tried to tenderly pry him out of the vehicle, and he took a drunken swing at me. His brother shook his head and we left him there hanging halfway out of the truck, like some virulent art piece.

I fell asleep again in the green recliner.

When I woke up his mother was sitting on the couch on the opposite wall watching the television and playing absentmindedly with the edge of her nightgown. His brother was in the kitchen and Kerry was gone in his truck. I went outside to smoke a cigarette and to feel less awkward. He returned while I was standing outside and gave me a sausage biscuit out of a white paper bag. "Helluva night, right?" he yelled, as I wordlessly accepted the package, "Let's hit the road!"

I thought we were headed back to Pascagoula, but instead we spent the latter part of the morning drinking more beer before Kerry showed his silent brother and I a natural dirt berm in a dried up lake bed near his mother's house. He called us pussies when we wouldn't ride in the bed while he ramped it in his truck. He crushed the front bumper pretty badly, split his head on the steering wheel, and screamed about it for a few minutes before he admitted defeat and we headed back to Pascagoula.

After we dropped his brother off, Kerry asked me to drive back to the coast. He slept the rest of the way, head bouncing on the passenger side window. Waking up on occasion to bitch about my cornering or turn up the radio for some obnoxious radio rock song.

When we got to the hotel, he promised that he would get me a new job, that he had all kinds of connections, and that he would take care of me. I never saw or heard from him again.

Illustration by Stephen Smith

Fibonacci for the Life List
Karla Linn Merrifield

The Amazon eco-tour sights
species of oddball
bird, odd poet
motmot-
like—
rare.

Going through a Period of Periods
Karla Linn Merrifield

I owe much to the period
of declarative sentences. It rained,
so I put on my socks. Periods that abet
description. Mr. Period punches gag
lines: Stella missed her period.
Old Polish joke. Grade-school days.
The period is adept at fragments
as well as minimalist basics, subject
plus verb equals: Euphemism sucks.
No wonder the period waxes imperious,
full of itself with imperatives.
Mind your manners. Beware of wolves.
Open the window. Make another rhyme.
Meanwhile, the period of abbrs.,
e.g., op.cit., ibid., plays hooky;
brb, btw, lol, etc.
Periods are plentiful.
I'll spare them not. Ever.
Instead, I time travel to Key West.
I seize ghostly periods
of Ernest Hemingway. The wind blows.
I write. Period. The end.

Offender
Christopher Lowe

Steven's wife set it in motion. She found the webpage. "Right down the street," she said. "Two doors down."

Caitlyn, their daughter, reached for the stuffed puppy Steven held. He was holding it out of her reach, just letting it dangle, and though it hurt him to do so, hurt him to listen to her fuss and squeal, he knew that it needed to be done, knew that what she needed was some motivation to stand. "What's there to do?"

"Something." Susan took the puppy from Steven, handed it to the child. "These people don't leave on their own." She went back to the computer. "His name's Warren."

Steven laid Caitlyn on her back. He held her ankles and bicycled her legs the way Dr. Forester had shown them. Caitlyn didn't squirm, didn't seem to mind anything he did to her legs.

"I can't find anything about the charges," Susan said.

"Maybe it wasn't anything major."

"Aren't they supposed to come around, introduce themselves so you know they live in your neighborhood?"

Steven stopped rotating Caitlyn's legs. He let go of the left and pulled on the right, extending it so that it was close to being straight. "I don't know."

"He was supposed to."

Steven pulled out the left, holding it out until Caitlyn started to fuss. He let go. The leg curled back. "I'll go talk to him, if it'll make you feel better."

Before she could argue, he'd handed Caitlyn off and was out the door. The night was turning cool. He'd left his shoes off, and he cut through the lawn of the vacant house that separated their home from Warren's.

He was nearly to the front walk when he stepped in the poop. It was runny, and the smell of it came to him immediately. He scrapped his foot across the grass and thought of the man inside, the man who had failed to clean up after his dog, who had, as Susan had pointed out, failed to come by and introduce himself.

He could still feel the mess between his toes when he climbed the steps to the porch and rapped on Warren's door. After a moment, the door opened and Warren stood there. He was more clean-cut than Steven had imagined.

"You need to pick up after your dog."

"It's my yard."

"This neighborhood, we pick up after our dogs."

"Look," the man said, "if you don't want to step in Franklin's business, don't walk in my yard."

Before he could do anything, Warren stepped back and let the door click shut.

Steven walked back down the porch and through the yard. He moved into the yard of the vacant house, and after a moment, he walked over to the realty sign that had been left there, untouched, for nearly a year. He leaned down, grabbed the post close to the ground and pulled. It slid free easily. He moved around the side of his own house, back to the shed, the sign cradled heavy in his arms.

The paint was right where he'd left it. Dark, rich purple, the only color he and Susan could agree on. He'd put primer on the walls, spent all morning doing it. They'd worked together on the painting, using rollers to layer and re-layer. When they were finished, when the walls were dry, they'd hung line drawings that Susan had done, pictures of boys and girls playing, kicking soccer balls, riding bicycles. One frame was larger than the others. It hung just above where Caitlyn's crib would go. The matte was scrawled over with more of Susan's drawings, kids running and jumping, tumbling over one another happily. In the center of all this was a photo from Susan's first ultrasound. Caitlyn, a bean still, huddled in the womb, no arms or legs, just a little oval of gray on a static-filled background. When the room was finished, they sat in the middle of it. He put his hand on Susan's belly. He kissed her shoulders, and she turned to him, slid her hand into the waistband of his shorts. They both knew that her back would hurt after, but they still made love there on the floor. When she came, Susan called out his name, and Steven remembered now how the words had echoed in the furniture-free room.

Steven used an old brush to scrawl the letters across the realty sign. He spaced them evenly, made them as neat as he could. He carried the sign to Warren's yard, drove it down into the soft earth using a rubber mallet. It made a loud thudding sound, like a basketball bouncing in an empty gym. He expected Warren to come out at any moment, roused by the noise, but he didn't.

When he was done, Steven walked out into the street. He'd angled the sign so that drivers could see it as they approached. SEX OFFENDER. He looked down at his hands, spackled with paint.

He closed his eyes, thought of Susan's line drawings, the picture framed in the center of them. His daughter, still unformed, still unbroken. He thought too of Dr. Forester saying in a calm voice, "These things just happen."

He imagined the bean growing as it must have, arms and legs shooting out, a head rising from the mass, fingers and toes and ears and all of it. He pictured her getting bigger, stronger, pictured her as one of Susan's drawings, strong, running hard after a soccer ball, a smile sprouted on her face.

He walked to the edge of the yard. He wanted Warren to come out, for there to be a confrontation. He wanted to go home with a black-eye, wanted Susan to hold ice-packs to his face, but he knew now that Warren wasn't coming out on his own. It was easier than he wanted to climb the man's steps, his fists clenched.

To the Trailer
Emily Porter

I.

It blew in with the moths
I caught in one motion between my fingers

and palm. A dusty October brood that skittered
across the hollyhocked window pane

and into my hands. Hands that loved the yard
until the grass was gone and that by November

shook and rolled like moths I couldn't catch, shook
like a small engine the pills would dismantle, reserved

for those who say *Damn the dog and the bitch neighbor
downstairs I'm about to burn this life to the ground* — an iron

hush that pocketed water in my face and tasted of burnt
citrus. I dreamt of sandbags, jetties, cedar log homes

my father had built. *Bulwarks and toothless jowls*, I told
the doctor. But the terrible bind is the dumb calm. I don't hear

vultures circle the meat in my mouth, just grace drain from my limbs,
the tenth street telephone pole peel the car frame from its axle and only

then my sister's lilt: *Enough. Come home.*

II.

I try to picture you but see our mother's face
the summer she and her sisters pulled us

from the jealous undertow. A child wrapped about
each hip, they dug in their heels and hauled us

toward the shore. The jellyfish blossomed, pearl-
dirty, pale

as the morning the moccasin slid in
the front door looking I imagine for a cool place

to sleep. Our falls rattled the hollow trailer floor.
After that, we kept the door closed, but

it always opens on our mother alone, that face.
Perhaps you've said to her *He's gone.* Some man. Perhaps

you'd believe if the words rose clay-singed
from the ground at the edge of the creek, at your

second wedding, where our father whispered
he could have been a better man. Her thin top lip

remembers each betrayal, every hound, buck,
mullet and maybe she said *Don't you get it, girl?* This

is how it is. Winter rubs one
unshaven leg against Spring: by March

you've turned the ground and dug your holes
around the doublewide's hem. Perennials.

Understand. What we crave is the eternal
return of the beloved. The sweat. The deafening bloom.

Vietnam. Fucking Vietnam
William Trent Pancoast

The darkness started on my lunch break at the fender factory. I went out by myself that day, late in February 1980 with snow on the ground, yet with full sunshine, the sort of day that promises something but you know it can't and won't deliver anything. I drove to the local beer dock where I bought the usual six pack then sat in the parking lot with the truck windows down, a cold breeze filtering through the cab.

Down a couple of spaces from me, one of the guys from shipping was sitting in his own pickup and playing Billy Joel's "Goodbye Saigon." He had it turned up loud like you're supposed to listen to that song, the anger of it shearing the hum of the factory in the distance. The song finished and he played it again, louder yet, the choppers, always the choppers in Vietnam, the fucking chopper war, blasting their rotors loud and obnoxious, the anger of the song blending with the arriving blackness of my mood, and it was 1966 again, us high school kids standing in the hallway looking at a picture of a guy who had graduated in the spring, just four months earlier. There on the bulletin board in the hallway was Tom Lane, a little guy, not athletic, not artistic or musical, not handsome, not anything that I could ever remember about him. But he was patriotic and dead. He had joined the Army and gone straight to Vietnam where he got blown up. So the school put his picture on the bulletin board in the main hallway, him kneeling in his fatigues holding his rifle and wearing his helmet, with a caption that read, "Tom Lane, killed in Vietnam last week." That day in the hallway was the first I had ever heard of Vietnam.

I sat there in the parking lot thinking of Tom Lane and the next year of 1967 when Vietnam was plastered all over the TV screen every evening, guys getting fucked up in front of us, and a great big What the Fuck was forming in my high school brain. I pictured my dad, the Army Infantry grunt from the Battle of the Bulge who got through the rest of his life by consuming a hundred thousand dollars worth of alcohol, watching the news, eyes fixed on the little black and white screen but flitting over to me every once in awhile like he wondered what the fuck I thought about it, or if I even understood what it was going to mean to me. He never talked to me about Vietnam—what I should do—join up, run, get a deferment, not a fucking thing.

The next year I was a student at Ohio State University. That winter I got a phone call that a friend in my class from high school had been killed in Nam. He had been there a week and stepped on a land mine. His wife was one month pregnant when he died.

I sat thinking these things and seeing these images, thinking too of the day of the Kent State killings when my dad and I came to blows, and a fierce dark anger covered me completely, the Vietnam War upon me again, a sickness that haunted every citizen in America those years—Johnson and Nixon and McNamara sending nearly three million American kids to a fucking worthless jungle just because they could, like the kings of old. Pick a country and make war. The darkness of all things settled over me that day at lunch in the parking lot of the GM plant and I didn't go back in the place.

I sat in the parking lot with nowhere to go now that I was back in the middle of the Vietnam War a half decade after the war's end. Back in the darkness, not going down together in Vietnam with my classmates and 58,200 others who got blown up, got sold out by the government, for the glory of nothing. For Nothing.

A whole country with PTSD—the American Legion guys hating the hippies, and the hippies hating the government, the government killing us all, and moms and dads and kids at every crossroad and in every corner of the nation in constant sorrow for the lost or soon to be lost children, and the governor of Ohio ordering the murder of kids at Kent State University.

I was plenty drunk, me and several of the regulars--Tony and Big Mike down at the end where they always sat and Crazy Jack three stools down from me--by the time John sat down on the bar stool beside me that evening. I could see that he was half in the bag too. "Hey. How's it going?" I asked.

He just nodded.

"I got this," I told the bartender.

John nodded again.

We drank our beers. I had heard that he was getting a divorce. Him and most of the other Vietnam guys. Treating their PTSD with alcohol like soldiers have done since alcohol was invented. But so was I getting a divorce. So was I sitting here.

"Where you working?" I asked him.

He tilted his head to look at me without turning his neck. "Nowhere man. There aren't any jobs." After a minute he added, "I think you got the last fucking job in America over at General Motors."

"Not much around," I said. I was past the darkness and way into the numbness and wanted everyone everywhere to be forgiven for everything and all get on with America and our lives.

"Your dad said he would get me in the plant. I can't even take care of my family."

"I'm sure he did what he could."

"He promised me. He said it was a sure thing he could get me in."

I imagined my dad sitting on a bar stool beside John up at the American Legion Hall, late in the evening and drunk, treating his own PTSD from 35 years ago and World War II.

"He said us vets got to stick together."

I nodded, starting to lapse back into the darkness from the numbness. "Man, it's hard to get anyone in that place."

"He got you in."

I glanced over at John, watched him rotate the beer bottle and pick at the label, the condensation dripping onto the bar.

"Yeah," I said. The darkness was back on top of the numbness and the anger of Vietnam was returning. I wanted to say I knew what he was feeling, but I didn't because I couldn't. I wanted to say that I was sorry I didn't go to Vietnam, but I wasn't.

"You got my fucking job."

"He did the best he could," I said, thinking of my old man, an accountant who had gotten fired in 1956 for standing up for vets where he worked then, when the company was firing them to beat them out of their retirement.

"Your old man's a fucking liar," he said.

"I don't think so," I told him.

"A fucking liar."

"Fuck you. Fucking Vietnam vet," I scoffed, all the anger and the darkness and numbness all rolled into one big ball of ugliness now.

He was to my right, so when I saw the first movement of his bar stool toward mine, I nailed him with a big roundhouse left hook and knocked him clean off his seat. He got up fast and I was ready, blind to everything except the enemy, and got him another good one. He socked me one hard punch in the eye, then the bartender pulled him off and Crazy Jack grabbed me. He held up his hands, palms out to indicate he was done, the dark sadness of the day on him too, and turned and headed for the door.

"What was that all about?" one of the guys asked.

"Vietnam. Fucking Vietnam."

The Kitchen Floor
Colleen Powderly

Chocolate poured on cement—that's the color of childhood.
Of the floor in the kitchen, where squabbles played out
across the table, by the stove. Where secrets
crystallized between raw shrimp in the freezer.
The floor covered with toys, shoes, spilled milk,
and Daddy's feet one day when I stepped on them—
he swore, yelled mine were too big.
Mama's miscarriage one Saturday morning while
he went on prayer retreat. He was easier after those,
she said, told him to go despite the cramping. She called
me from cartoons to clean up blood. I was nine,
oldest, calming the others while I soaked
old towels, rinsed them in the toilet like diapers.
The next summer, expecting Daddy's Yankee family,
Mama waxed that floor to a glossy shine. Fed up
by extra work, she grumbled. I parroted. She slid
across the floor then, bare feet skidding, begging him
to stop slapping her. My brother stood on the floor
near Thanksgiving that year, naked to the waist
while she salved belt buckle cuts on his back.
That floor held us all once or twice, eight people
walking, skidding, falling accidentally or by design,
along with blackeyed peas, dropped chicken bones,
cornbread crumbs, and greasy French fries.
Its chocolate colluded with my childhood
confusion, made pictures I still wake to see.

Ax
Esteban Rodriguez

Even after all the scrubbing, the scent of wood stayed ripe around my hands, the handle of a crooked ax, hot and splintered as I'd tightly grip the belly, hew log after log after log after log; no gloves or goggles, no time to think about the way friction reshaped my fingerprints, how easy wood split from wood if I didn't question my quota, if I believed anger could be sanctioned into cathartic action, too focused not to know what I was actually doing, this backyard chore my father put me to work on every weekend. He'd say that we all needed to learn 'the lesson,' discipline before duty, duty before knowing what it meant to work in this world for a living. And I'd sometimes think these had to be bad hallucinations, since my father never spoke in metaphors, never lectured beyond simple body language, a grunt as he'd hand me the ax, and I went to work wedging the blade through bark, through rings, through hours of the hickory haft melting into my palms; my daydreams fueled by heat, as I'd become a miner, firefighter, a lumberjack who chiseled the wood into a different type of meaning, giving me a reason to construct a cabin inside my head, chop and store all these afternoons inside of it, and wait for my skin to shed the scent of log I'd toss into a pile like bones, a feeling I could almost claim as guilt, not knowing my father saw this work as rite, every back bent back and swing swung down as a see-saw for balance he'd imagine I'd find, as I imagined myself naked inside this cabin, stripped of purpose and ready to harvest my blisters deep inside these woods.

Calf
Esteban Rodriguez

The moon swings down from its morning socket, and a horde of flies swarm the eyes of the calf garroted between the barbed-wire fence, her squeals sharper than the echoes from her birth, as she now struggles to untangle herself from this womb of a mess; legs and neck rusted by the teeth digging further through her flesh, as I dig my fingers through her sticky hair, pull her spine closer to my chest. She's trembling as if this were winter, and I imagine snow quilted on our heads, flakes draped above the yawning hills, soft and thin, and more a reason to believe I can find innocence in this event, that she won't remember the severity of her wounds, and I'll tread back home lending my father a quiet hand. But the wire's webbed around her skin like fate, and she's slowing down the pace on her kicks and jumps, as I'm carving stigmata on my humid palms, aware God is far from this horizontal crucifixion, that the sacrifice here isn't meant to be prophetic, but practical, a chance to resurrect her growing silence into a silence of afternoon grazing, so she can linger the way cows have perfected the act of lingering, and I can watch this from a distance, convinced even the bruised sky will heal itself.

Cats
Esteban Rodriguez

Belly blacker than asphalt, than fresh tire marks and the silhouette of mesquite against a filmstrip sky, I squat down as if to pay tribute, an amateur in animal deaths, in stray cats I feed dinner-scraps against my mother's will. These are the driveway scavengers, solicitors of sympathy rubbing against my leg, and this one is the dead one that veered off its map, tested traffic, briefly became brave. I study the lump of feral bone and flesh, how the miscellany of its stomach spreads out like scree, red, rotten, rumpled like morning bed sheets, and there is a sense that if I believe in fate, this is the only end the cat could have endured, that my being here is a kind of funeral, and my silence a roadside elegy for all the lives this stretch of road has ever killed. I feel I should toss it back in the yard, prepare a more human ritual, but my hands are too young to dig a proper burial, work through dusk and watch the suburban moon rise into our country air, as it becomes a witness to the after-act of death again, and I scrape my shovel beneath its head instead, dump it in a nearby bush, turn back home with the hum of 281 singing in my ears.

Ghost
Anna Lowe Weber

October came gold as a dried worm,
sidewalk-fried in the last days of heat. We forgot
how the South could hold summer in its teeth
like a dog who's caught what he's been after,
crunching those delicate bones, refusing to drop it.
That month was a minefield of fallen skies
and the simper of streetlamps. We were always
on our way back from something, pulling
into the driveway at dusk. Sitting in the car
to observe our new blue house, the clean lines,
the drying hydrangeas, how the windows
lit from within stank of some rotten spirit
we'd not shake for years.

Contributors

Cathy Adams spent the first twenty years of her life in Alabama, about twenty more in Georgia and North Carolina, and now she lives and writes in Xinzheng, China. Her short stories have won numerous awards such as the Mona Schreiber Award for Humorous Fiction and a National Public Radio Director's award. She has short stories scheduled for publication in *A River and Sound Review, Bete Noire, Ontologica,* and *Cha: An Asian Literary Journal*. Her first novel, *This is What It Smells Like*, was recently published by New Libri Press, Washington.

Lis Anna is a 2011 Pushcart Prize nominee and the recipient of many awards including a five time WorldFest winner, FadeIn, Telluride IndieFest winner, Helene Wurlitzer Grant recipient, Chesterfield Film Project Finalist, New Century Writers winner and a finalist in the prestigious William Faulkner Competition. Her short films, screenplays, and novels have all been nominated and subsequently won awards including Best Novel and Best Short Film. She is the 2011 Readers Choice Award recipient from Fiction Fix and the Second Place 2011 Winner of the Hint Fiction Contest. Her fiction has been published in *Word Riot, The Blotter, Petigru Review, Hot Metal Press, The Smoking Poet, Eclectic Flash Literary Journal, Paper Skin Glass Bones, 491 Magazine, Fiction Fix, The Monarch Review, 5×5 Literary Magazine, Red Booth Review, Hint Fiction Anthology, Chamber Four Literary Magazine, Emrys Journal, Literary Laundry, Barely South Review, Flash Fiction Offensive, Flashquake Literary Journal,* and *The MacGuffin Literary Review*.

CL Bledsoe is the author of five novels including the young adult novel *Sunlight*, the novels *Last Stand in Zombietown* and *$7.50/hr + Curses*; four poetry collections: *Riceland, _____(Want/Need), Anthem,* and *Leap Year*; and a short story collection called *Naming the Animals*. He has two poetry chapbooks available online: *Goodbye to Noise* and *The Man Who Killed Himself in My Bathroom*. He's been nominated for the Pushcart Prize eight times, had two stories selected as Notable Stories by Story South's Million Writers Award and two others nominated, and has been nominated for Best of the Net twice. He's also had a flash story selected for the long list of Wigleaf's 50 Best Flash Stories award. He blogs at *Murder Your Darlings*. Bledsoe reviews regularly for *Rain Taxi, Coal Hill Review, Prick of the Spindle, Monkey Bicycle, Book Slut, The Hollins Critic, The Arkansas Review, American Book Review, The Pedestal Magazine,* and elsewhere. Bledsoe lives with his wife and daughter in Maryland.

Justin J. Brouckaert is the author of the chapbook *Look at this Fish* (Burning River Press, April 2014), a collection of flash fiction and prose poetry. He is a James Dickey Fellow in Fiction at the University of South Carolina.

Katie Burgess earned her PhD in creative writing at Florida State University, where she received the Robert Olen Butler Fiction Dissertation Award. She resides in her mother-in-law's dining room.

Maari Carter is originally from Winona, MS and attended The University of Mississippi where she received a B.A. in English. She is currently pursuing an M.F.A. in Creative Writing at Florida State University.

Tobi Cogswell is a multiple Pushcart nominee and a Best of the Net nominee. Credits include or are forthcoming in various journals in the US, UK, Sweden and Australia. In 2012 and 2013 she was short-listed for the Fermoy International Poetry Festival. In 2013 she received Honorable Mention for the Rachel Sherwood Poetry Prize. Her sixth and latest chapbook is *Lapses & Absences* (Blue Horse Press). She is the co-editor of *San Pedro River Review*.

Jackson Culpepper grew up in south Georgia and now lives in east Tennessee with his wife Margaret, two dogs, and two horses. His work has appeared in *Armchair/Shotgun*, *Rock & Sling*, *The Drum Literary Magazine*, and *Real South Magazine*.

John Davis, Jr.'s poetic work has been published in venues internationally, with recent appearances in *Deep South Magazine*, *Saw Palm*, *Real South*, and *Floyd County Moonshine*, among other fine literary outlets. In 2012, he was among the winners of the Robert Frost Poetry and Haiku Contest, sponsored by the Studios of Key West. His poetry has also been nominated for the Pushcart Prize.

Tyler Dennis is a fifth-year senior at the University of Alabama at Birmingham. When he's not writing, he's boxing pizzas for $7.75 an hour at a pizza joint in Southside Birmingham.

After a rather extended and varied second childhood in New Orleans (street musician, psych-tech, riverboat something-or-other, door-to-door poetry peddler, etc.), **Matt Dennison** finished his undergraduate degree at Mississippi State University where he won the National Sigma Tau Delta essay competition (judged by X.J. Kennedy). His work has appeared in *Rattle*, *Natural Bridge*, *The Spoon River Poetry Review*, and *Cider Press Review*, among others. He currently lives in a 108-year-old house with "lots of potential."

Michael Diebert is poetry editor for *The Chattahoochee Review* and teaches writing and literature at Georgia Perimeter College in Atlanta. He is the author of *Life Outside the Set*, available from Sweatshoppe Publications. Other recent work has appeared in *Flycatcher, jmww*, and *The Dead Mule School of Southern Literature*.

Brenna Dixon is a native Floridian with an MFA in Creative Writing and Environment from Iowa State University, where she teaches Composition and Fiction. Her fiction, nonfiction, and lit journal reviews can be found in *The Southeast Review, South Dakota Review, Burrow Press Review*, and *The Review Review*. You can also find her work over at *Ploughshares*, where she is a 2013 Blogger. She's putting the finishing touches on a collection of short stories called *Sawgrass and the Broken Heart*, and will return to her native land as a 2014 Artist-in-Residence at Everglades National Park.

Mario Duarte lives in Iowa City, Iowa and is a graduate of the Iowa Writers' Workshop. Recently, he has recently published poems in the *Acentos Review, Broken Plate, Huizache, Shadowbox*, and *Slab*, and has work forthcoming in *Dicho* and *Passages North*.

Lauren Eyler is from Cape Hatteras, North Carolina. She received her MFA from the University of South Carolina. She has been published in *The Rumpus Saint Anne's Review, Bluestem*, and other journals. The primary colors are red, yellow, blue.

Brandi George grew up in rural Michigan. Her first collection of poetry, *Gog*, is forthcoming from Black Lawrence Press in 2015. Poems from this manuscript have appeared in such journals as *Gulf Coast, Prairie Schooner, Best New Poets 2010*, and *The Iowa Review*. She currently resides in Tallahassee, where she is a PhD candidate at Florida State University, Assistant to the Director of Creative Writing, and editor of *The Southeast Review*.

Deborah Gold is the pseudonym of a writer, teacher, and foster parent.

Hastings Hensel is the author of a chapbook, *Control Burn*, which won the Iron Horse Literary Review's 2011 Single-Author Contest, and his poetry and non-fiction have appeared in numerous journals and magazines, including *Shenandoah, The Hopkins Review, New South, Birmingham Poetry Review, Gray's Sporting Journal, 32 Poems, The Greensboro Review*, and others.

Jody Hobbs Hesler lives in the foothills of the Blue Ridge Mountains. Her work has appeared or is forthcoming in *Stealing Time: A Literary Magazine For Parents, Valparaiso Fiction Review, Prime Number, Pearl, The Blue Ridge Anthology, Writer's Eye Anthology, Potato Eyes Journal, Leaf Garden Press, Charlottesville Family Magazine*, and *A Short Ride: Remembering Barry Hannah*, a VOX Press tribute anthology.

Ian Hoppe is a writer, draftsman, musician, and electrician in Birmingham, Alabama. He is a contributor to *The Birmingham Free Press* and a blogger for al.com. He also works for a local engineering firm as an AutoCAD operator, plays with Birmingham based Irish-pub group Jasper Coal, and dabbles in computer science.

Donald Illich's work has been published in *The Iowa Review*, *Nimrod*, *Cream City Review*, and several other journals.

Christopher Lowe is the author of *Those Like Us: Stories* (SFASU Press, 2011). His fiction, non-fiction, and poetry have appeared widely in journals including *Third Coast*, *Bellevue Literary Review*, *Grist*, *Barely South Review*, *Baltimore Review*, and *War, Literature, and the Arts*. He is an assistant fiction editor for *Fifth Wednesday Journal*. A native of Mississippi, he lives with his wife and daughter in Lake Charles, LA, where he teaches English and Creative Writing at McNeese State University.

Ray McManus is the author of three books of poetry: *Driving Through the Country Before You are Born* (USC Press 2007), *Left Behind* (Steeping Stones Press 2008), and *Red Dirt Jesus* (Marick Press 2011). His poetry has appeared in many journals most recently: *Natural Bridge*, *Barely South*, *Pea River Review*, *The Pinch*, *Hayden's Ferry*, and *moonShine Review*. Ray is the creative writing director for the Tri-District Arts Consortium in South Carolina, and he is an Assistant Professor of English in the Division of Arts and Letters at University of South Carolina Sumter where he teaches creative writing, Irish literature, and Southern literature.

Claire McQuerry's collection of poetry, *Lacemakers*, was winner of the Crab Orchard First Book award, and her poems and essays have appeared in *Mid-American Review*, *Louisville Review*, *Western Humanities Review*, and other journals.

A seven-time Pushcart-Prize nominee and National Park Artist-in-Residence, **Karla Linn Merrifield** has had some 400 poems appear in dozens of journals and anthologies. She has ten books to her credit, the newest of which are *Lithic Scatter and Other Poems* (Mercury Heartlink) and *Attaining Canopy: Amazon Poems* (FootHills Publishing). Forthcoming from Salmon Poetry is *Athabaskan Fractal and Other Poems of the Far North*. Her *Godwit: Poems of Canada* (FootHills) received the 2009 Eiseman Award for Poetry, and she recently received the Dr. Sherwin Howard Award for the best poetry published in *Weber – The Contemporary West* in 2012. She is assistant editor and poetry book reviewer for *The Centrifugal Eye* (www.centrifugaleye.com), a member of the board of directors of TallGrass Writers Guild and Just Poets (Rochester, NY), and a member of the New Mexico State Poetry Society.

William Trent Pancoast's novels include *Wildcat* (2010) and *Crashing* (1983). His short stories, essays, and editorials have appeared in *MONKEYBICYCLE*, *Night Train*, *The Mountain Call*, *Solidarity Magazine*, and *US News & World Report*. Pancoast recently retired from the auto industry after thirty years as a die maker and union newspaper editor. Born in 1949, the author lives in Ontario, Ohio. He has a BA in English from the Ohio State University.

Born in Texas, **Colleen Powderly** lived in Louisiana before moving to Rochester with her family when she was 12. After receiving her MA in 1997, she worked at a number of full and part-time jobs, finishing with a three-year stint as a prison counselor. Her work reflects her Southern childhood as well as the struggle she experienced and witnessed while trying to make a living. Her work has appeared in *HazMat Review*, *Fox Cry Review*, *The Palo Alto Review*, *RiverSedge*, *Sea Stories*, *MG2Datura*, *The Weekly Avocet*, and *The Centrifugal Eye*.

Emily Porter is a native of North Florida. She earned an MFA from the University of Virginia.

Esteban Rodríguez holds an MFA from the University of Texas Pan-American, and works as an elementary reading and writing tutor in the Rio Grande Valley, promoting both English and Spanish literacy. His poetry is forthcoming in *The Los Angeles Review*, *storySouth*, *The Country Dog Review*, and *Huizache*. He lives in Weslaco, Texas.

Originally from Louisiana, **Anna Lowe Weber** currently lives in Huntsville, Alabama, where she teaches creative writing and composition for the University of Alabama in Huntsville. Her work has appeared or is forthcoming in the *Florida Review*, *Blue Mesa Review*, and *Rattle*, among others.